JAMES SHORE'S DAUGHTER

WORKS OF

STEPHEN VINCENT BENÉT

James Shore's Daughter
Ballads and Poems 1915–1930
Heavens and Earth
Young Adventure
John Brown's Body
Tiger Joy
Jean Huguenot
Spanish Bayonet
Young People's Pride
Five Men and Pompey
The Beginning of Wisdom

BY

ROSEMARY AND STEPHEN VINCENT BENÉT
A Book of Americans

STEPHEN VINCENT BENÉT

James Shore's Daughter

MCMXXXIV
Doubleday, Doran & Company, Inc.
Garden City, New York

PRINTED AT THE *Country Life Press*, GARDEN CITY, N. Y., U. S. A.

To Richard *and* Alice Lee Myers
With Affection

PART I

My MOTHER had a memory book for each of us, in those days, and they traveled with us over the face of the earth. There was the Book of Enid and the Book of Imogen, the Book of Carlo, and mine. I hadn't seen it for years, but, as soon as I opened the package, I remembered. They were all rather shakily bound in genuine Florentine leather, and Mother did the tooling herself. The *fleur-de-lis* and the stars are a little uncertain, and the Grecian urns look singularly like coffee pots. But, at that, they have lasted better than the illuminated page

[*3*]

headings. Miss Paget did those, in water colors. She also did ferns.

The First Smile—The First Walk—The First Christmas—all are there. Enid's, as I remember it, had a little cardboard socket for the First Tooth, but then, she was the eldest. And toward the rear of Enid's there is a heading, "The First Masterpiece." Miss Paget didn't do that. It is scrolled in the dashing, familiar hand that used three exclamation points to a sentence and never was tired of underlining words.

Poor Mother, she did so want her children to be geniuses! She did not specify the subject of Enid's masterpiece, but I know she saw it, at the Salon, in a very large gilt frame. The corresponding page in mine is a little less confident. It merely says "The First Public Concert," and there is no straggling vine of laurel twining about the letters. But I was six years younger than Enid, and life had told on Mother by then. She named me Gareth and let it go at that. It was to have been Pompilia, if I had been a girl.

And underneath the bold headings are blankness and a few flyspecks and the yellowed look of paper that wasn't real parchment after all. The real

[4]

events—the real touchstones of life—were elsewhere. I heard so much great music when I was a
child. And I remember the hand organ in the Bois,
one sunny morning, and the croak of Punch's
trumpet in a London square. Likewise, when I
think of majesty, I do not think of the horned
Moses or God in the Sistine Chapel. I think,
automatically, of the landlady who kept the third-
class private hotel at Folkestone, when I was six.
It rained, and she wore black silk, and, when she
watered the aspidistra, you could hear the whole
British Empire creak with her stays. And so, when
I think of my own birthright, I still think of Violet
Shore.

It was the winter we spent in New York—the
brownstone winter in the house on Thirty-sixth
Street that Mrs. Alstyne lent us. After all, as
Mother explained, we were Father's legacy to his
country, and, now the girls were getting big, it was
really our duty to come home. America needed
leaven, and the torch must be carried on. We must
be gentle with America, gentle but firm. It was
our motherland, though it hadn't bought Father's
pictures.

She read us "Prospice" and "Captain, O My

[5]

Captain" and we all felt very enthusiastic, thinking of America. We looked forward to a future of Indians and ice-cream sodas and the children we'd read about in *St. Nicholas*—the healthy, self-reliant children named Donald and Dorothy who lived in big, wooden houses with benevolent uncles—the ragged but still self-reliant and healthy children who slept in packing boxes but weren't *lazzaroni*, like Teddy and Carrots, the Young Merchants of Newspaper Row. Silver watches, ponies, and adventures fairly rained upon American children but never spoiled them—they were too democratic for that. They were always frank and rosy and humorous, and any one of them could make a practical ice boat out of a chicken coop. True, there had as yet been no serial in *St. Nicholas* called "The Young Prodigies, or The Grant Family Rediscovers America." But we felt this was a remediable oversight. We could write it ourselves as soon as we really got back.

It seems a little pathetic, in retrospect. Understand, it was all our fault—we were really insufferable little toads. A prodigy is bad enough, but to have the tricks of the prodigy without the talent! The eager, enormous vanity, the professional air,

[6]

the catch phrase, the mock modesty, the charming little touch of gaucheness that tells so well with the audience—we knew them all. No wonder the Donalds and Dorothys sniffed us and let us alone. Even Carlo, at six, recited with the glib, appalling smoothness of the "gifted amateur." And as for Enid's painting and Imogen's dancing and my fiddle! I can see myself, in the Fauntleroy suit, with bow professionally poised, as the ladies' dresses rustled and the audience settled down. I can see myself, I say. But, fortunately, at this distance, I cannot hear.

We were used to being queer and a clan, we were horribly used to carrying on the torch. But, in Europe, we could tell ourselves that we were Americans and superior. To be queer in America itself was merely hateful. We had no defense against the frank, good-humored children, or their frank, good-humored fun. Enid had the best of it, for teachers always liked Enid. They would look at her and quote Tennyson, especially "The Princess." She had a great deal of blonde hair and Father's forehead, and Mother usually introduced her as "my little Saxon maid." But even Enid was not a real success at Miss Pierce's—at least with her own contemporaries. They got tired of being told that it was a privilege to have her in the school. And the rest of us were rather decided failures. Carlo did well enough, to be sure, at the model kindergarten till he discovered that "dago" was a term of reproach. Then he hit two boys on the head with the First Gift and promised to remove their livers as soon as he could get a knife. He had picked up quite a lot of colloquial Tuscan, and it didn't sound well, translated. I imagine the Finchley sisters were relieved when he started a series of colds and had to be kept at home.

For even the lush steam heat that we reveled in, at first, betrayed us. We were used to the cold grue of Italian pensions, out of season, when the tramontana bent the tops of the poplars; to the chilblained stones of French courtyards; to warming our purple fingers in front of the three damp coals of a British fire. And now, when, for the first time in our lives, we were warm in winter, we began to sniffle and wheeze. The arid blast from the registers—dusty and incessant as the talk of the ladies from Browning Societies who came to call on Mother—made us gasp like stranded goldfish. I know that, for a long time afterwards, I could not think of New York without feeling a distinct dryness at the back of my nose.

Even for Mother, the dream began to fade. Oh, her old friends remembered her and were kind. But they liked to remember Kitty Antwerp, the girl who eloped with the artist with the silky brown beard. The legend brought a glint of warm Roman sun into the draped and massive drawing rooms where the light seemed always brown, it touched the heavy silver of the solid tea services with an adventurous ray. But Kitty Antwerp, fifteen years later, with four children and such odd ideas, was different. Remarkably talented children, of course, but still . . . It was all very well to talk about the Medicis and the sacred flame, but Kitty seemed to expect so much and so definitely. Dolly's last year's coat would do nicely for the second girl, and the little boy's music lessons could be arranged for. But no one seemed really interested in carrying on the torch.

I didn't know all this at the time—a child doesn't. I just knew that my underwear scratched and that I wished we were back in Europe. It seemed beautiful, in retrospect, even to some of the rather horrid trips we'd taken for Mother's

[*9*]

Jaunty series. *A Jaunty Heart in Cornwall, A Jaunty Heart in Normandy*—I don't know if you've ever seen them, in second-hand bookstores. They were among the first of the really chatty guidebooks—the kind that lead you from beauty to beauty with a warm, moist friendly hand. But they hadn't come to their success yet, and all we children knew was the singular discomfort of living in quaint places.

Nevertheless, even the fishy little cottage at Penzance grew bright in recollection now, for the pictures in *St. Nicholas* had failed me, and the gaseous splendors of ice-cream soda didn't make up for the rest. And then came the afternoon at Mrs. Harvester's. Ostensibly, it was merely a party for Jane Harvester, but Mother had seized upon it as her last and greatest attempt to deal with America firmly. We were definitely on show— all four of us—and there were others. Seedlings of genius, exhibited under glass. I remember a knobby girl named Madeleine MacKenzie Moore who re- cited poems about gnomes, poems that she herself had written. She was the only other certified prod- igy, but there were others whose parents hoped.

When my number was over, I managed to slip

away through the confusion of the improvised greenroom and down the back stairs. I was hot, and I knew that when the refreshments did come I'd have to help pass them and be talked to. But there were men in the kitchen, and the cook wasn't friendly at all, though there seemed to be lots of ice cream. So I was taken back through the dining room and left on the edge of the audience. I couldn't see the stage, but I knew it was Imogen dancing from the firm thud of feet on the boards. Then a hand beckoned me from the landing of the front stairs, and it was Violet Shore.

She was eight years old and defiantly solid and healthy. She had on a frilly white dress and a pin that sparkled, and her long black-stockinged legs were not like the legs of European children. But, even then, she had those enormous eyes. I stood there, pulling at my Fauntleroy collar. I was used to little girls being much too strong, in America, but I had never seen a little girl quite like this one. She looked like a person, and most of them merely looked strong.

"Hello, boy," she said briefly. "Your collar's dirty. I don't think this is a nice party. Get me some ice cream."

[*11*]

"Get it yourself," I said. "You're not supposed to sit on those stairs, anyway. It's the Harvesters' house."

"As if I didn't know," she said and yawned. "Smarty," she added with a grin.

"Smarty yourself," I said, with a sudden warm feeling of companionship. "Smarty gave a party."

"It isn't my party," she said. "I have magicians at my parties. Magicians as big as this house."

"I bet you do," I said. "I bet you have lions and tigers, too."

"I bet I could if I wanted," she said placidly. I sat down beside her, and a silence fell between us.

"Did you hear me play?" I said. "Everybody thinks I play awfully well."

"I don't," she said. "It all sounds squally to me."

"That's the tone color," I said. "That's what you call it—tone color. Where were you born? I was born in Rome, and I've got two sisters and a brother, and we're all very talented. Everybody knows that."

"I've got a brother," she said. "And he can fight and swear. I bet he could lick you if he wanted. Come on, let's get some ice cream."

"You can't," I said. "There are lots of men with suits in the kitchen."

"Oh, they're just waiters," she said. "They don't matter to anybody. And the cook'll say 'Yes, Miss Violet.' You'll see."

I followed her, doubtingly, but it was as she had said, even to the mechanical smiles on the waiters' faces. I marveled, hoping she did not see the marvel, but she did.

"It's always that way," she deigned to explain. "I always get what I want. You see, my father's rich. He's the richest man in the world, I guess. So I always get what I want."

"My father was a great artist," I said, feebly. "He painted pictures, like dear Leonardo and gay Raffaello." I trilled the Italian deliberately.

"Huh," she said. "They sound like organ grinders. Your father was an organ grinder."

"He was not," I said. "He was great. And, anyhow, he's dead."

She looked at me a moment.

"I'm sorry," she said, in a curiously low and moving voice for a child. "There isn't much you can do when people are dead."

"No," I said, suddenly miserable, though I had

no particularly poignant memories of Father. "There isn't." I kicked one foot with the other one.

"Listen," she said. "Aleck's got a train with real engines. You can come and play with it. They'll let you in. I'll tell Roberts."

"Thanks," I said, still kicking my shoe. I knew I was doing it now, but that didn't help. I was suddenly overwhelmed by the absolute, reasonless misery of a child. The ice cream was there on my plate, but I did not want to eat it. I was talented and knew all about dear Leonardo and my father had been a great artist and nothing good would ever happen to me again.

"Listen," she said, finally. "Would you like to kiss me? I don't care if you do."

I looked at her, blankly. There were those enormous eyes and the face like a hardy flower.

"Not much," I said. "Why would I?"

"Oh, I don't know," she said. "But sometimes when Father's sad, he kisses somebody and then he feels better. It used to be Mother, but now sometimes it's Miss Wheelock. Mother's dead, too, you know. There were lots of flowers and a man in a black dress."

"Has your brother's train got a drawbridge?"

I said. "I could kiss your hand if you wanted me to. People do that, abroad. They think it's fancy."

"All right," she said, and I took her hand and kissed it, remembering Guido in Rome. He was a fat little man, but a Count, and he kissed Mother's hand with rotund and formal solemnity, whenever he came to call. I did my best to imitate the neat bob of his head and failed. And this hand didn't smell like Mother's, of orange-flower soap. But it was the first time I touched American earth.

Violet looked at me afterwards with a queer, adult puzzlement.

"I don't see why they do it," she said. "Except for being fancy. But I said I didn't mind and I don't. What's your name?"

I told her—and the display of seedlings ended with Carlo—and then I was haled away to help Madeleine MacKenzie Moore pass the cakes.

I saw Violet across the room, later. There were other little girls with her, all frilly-dressed and black-stockinged, but she was still different from them. "So that's the little Shore," said a voice behind me. "Sarah loves to experiment, doesn't she?" Another voice said, "Oh, she's quite a well-mannered little thing. And, after all, my dear . . ."

[*15*]

There was something in the voices I could not quite place—a mingling of sharpness and unwilling respect—as if the name were magic and they did not like its being magic. But for me, even then, the magic was not in the name.

All the same, she was James Shore's daughter, and Mother soon found it out. Before that, my chief consolation had been the open New York Central tracks. I used to wander up there, when I was left alone. Park Avenue had not yet been roofed over, behind the station, and you could look down on the very roofs of the cars. There was a great deal of noise and the black taste of smoke and cinders and the long disheveled trains, so much bigger than European ones, coming in from the length and breadth of a continent that took six days to cross. I could listen to them and forget that I was strange and bound to be a genius to make up for Father's pictures. And it didn't matter any more what Mother wanted from the heavy ladies in black satin and the dried, half-English men. The true gods of the land were moguls and eight-wheeled compounds and men with grease on their faces and the light, fierce mountain engines that climbed, somewhere, the interminable grades of the West. I was only ten and not up to making phrases, but I felt a roaring power and an un-acknowledged beauty—a barbarous thing with a certain simplicity of heart. And, when I began going often to Violet's house, I knew somehow that she and the trains were akin.

The carriage would stop at Thirty-sixth Street, and the stiff white note would be left and Mother would try to remember about my nails. Then the man would get down to open the carriage door for me, as I came down the steps. The house on Sixty-second was only three years built then and far up-town. James Shore's wife had liked the air and the openness there, though she didn't live to enjoy them. It was quite a long drive in the carriage, but I always relished it. I'd sit back with my hands clasped and pretend they were my horses, and now and then I'd nod gravely to some grown-ups on the sidewalk, just to see them stare and hur-riedly become polite. An unnatural little snob? Perhaps, but it was something on a clear afternoon, the Avenue before the automobiles. You could see New York and feel it, beside you, like a running torrent. Now the torrent is over your head.

The house itself didn't particularly impress me,

except for the elevator, which you worked by pulling a plush-colored rope. I thought it was very grand and like a palace, but, after all, I'd seen palaces, and the marble statues in the hall just looked like things in museums. It was the servants who made my ears feel hot. I never was easy with them and they knew it—servants of that sort are like horses, they know in a minute whether you have the gift. And I never was particularly easy with Aleck Shore. He was just my age, but already he looked like a young, handsome bull. We had to fight and we did, and after that he was better. But, except for the train, we never really got on. He had another thing already, that enormous arrogance of the rich—an arrogance so vast and unconscious that it seems like a natural force. It lies underneath the good manners, and you don't often touch it. But, when you do, it has none of the warmth and gayety of vanity. It is cold as the front-hall marbles; cold as steel and stone.

It was an eerie place for children to play in, that house. Everything was either brand-new or warranted antique, like the marbles—but, in either case, there was no sense of continuance, such as you find in most houses—it might all have been bought overnight at one great auction and the vans come with it the next day. And, to a child's eyes, it was all like some vast, rich jungle, crowded with soft, deep carpets and hothouse plants and hundreds of little gimcracks in china and bronze and silver that swarmed upon tables and huddled into glass-fronted cabinets and got dusted and broken and lost without ever getting any fewer. There were endless toys in the nursery, but we played with few of them, except the train. We preferred the library, where even James Shore never came and you could play the tortures of the Spanish Inquisition with a monkey wrench and a pair of pliers and be sure that the screams of the tortured would not be heard upstairs. Aleck liked to bully, but he couldn't bully us both.

Outside and around and beyond lay the city and the land and the time, and those, too, I remember. It all mixes together in memory, the tangle of wires on the telegraph poles and the squirrels in the Park and the look of block after block of identical brownstone. In the streets were the old policemen in big helmets, the barrel-bellied policemen with Cleveland mustaches, the policemen that are gone. There were horsecars and

[*19*]

Pyle's Pearline and a man with a lemonade cart, and when the great blizzard came the streets looked like ice caves, and, after it, there were hundreds and hundreds of sleighs. I remember all that, and more. I remember the dirty-faced boy who yelled, "Take de flies out of yer ears!" at me, and the little engines on the Elevated. I have seen books since, recalling these things as quaint, and they have made me feel odd. For they assume that I knew I was living in an epoch, and, of course, I did not know.

I did not know, but I felt something in my skin. If it hadn't been for Violet, I would have been as frankly disappointed and homesick as the others. We never got to the frontier, we never even got to the New England landscape where the little boys of Miss Alcott went nutting, in round jackets, with red mufflers about their throats. But I knew that these things existed, because of a girl with black-stockinged legs who would fight before she would cry. I can see her still against a confused background of steam heat and high stoops and sparrows and buildings that then seemed tall—and there is a queer innocence to the picture.

It all got to be a part of my life so quickly. A

sheltered child might have been dazzled or envious, but I was neither. At least Mother did that much for us. I accepted the mansion on Sixty-second Street as I had accepted the Folkestone boarding house—it was the way things were at Violet's and that was all. Sometimes we went to the Park and there were other children, but the times I remember best were the times that we played alone. There was a tall, faded lady in beautiful clothes called Aunt Amy who smelt of Hoyt's German Cologne and was supposed to mother Violet, but we never paid much attention to her. There were maids who were either enemies or friends. And there was the butler, Roberts, whom even Aleck respected— a quiet, stocky man with an eye that could blaze like a coal.

Aleck, when he had the chance, would follow him around like a dog. I can still hear the voices from the butler's pantry, the spoiled voice saying, "Aw, Roberts, lemme help you clean the silver," and the firm one, "No, Master Aleck. That is my place, not yours. Besides, you have a guest."

"Aw, Roberts, he's not *my* guest . . ."

"Always tagging!" Violet would mutter, under her breath. "Always tagging after the *servants!*"

But she didn't dare say it out loud. James Shore was well served, in Roberts. He wasn't always so well served.

He'd come back sometimes toward evening, James Shore, when I'd stayed to supper, and stand in the door, tall and silent, with his black beard thrust ahead of him and a white, wrapped parcel in his hand. A still man, dressed in hard, expensive cloth, with the big nose of the conqueror. Then Violet would run to him, and he'd pull her ears. Once, I remember, he sat down at the table with us and pretended he was a prospector who had been snowed in all winter in the Rockies and had just come back to town. It was a terrifyingly life-like impersonation. But generally, as soon as they had opened the parcel, he'd go away.

I thought him a nice man, on the whole, but unaccountable. He always called me "the Colonel," as if it were a joke between us, but I didn't know the joke and it made me feel shy. He was the one thing or being you couldn't tease Violet about. They never seemed to have much to say to each other, but you could feel a current running between them, as if they were copper, say, and the rest of the world were glass.

[22]

There were formal calls exchanged between Mother and Aunt Amy, but Violet came only once to Thirty-sixth Street, and the others never went with me to Sixty-second. I was just as glad, on the whole. It wasn't all jealousy, though that entered in. I knew, somehow, it wouldn't work. And Mother wanted me to play for Mr. Shore, but I didn't do that till the end. You see, I was in love. You can't be in love at ten? Very well, you can't.

I don't remember falling in love. I remember slapping Imogen because she called Violet stuck up, and having to apologize later—and feeling uncomfortable at certain things Mother said. They weren't meant for me, but I overheard them, as children will—no grown person has ever remembered how much a child overhears. "Yes, Gareth is going to see his little friend," and a casual allusion to the Shores. Then the caller would look at me with a certain kind of smile, and she and Mother would immediately begin to talk about something called changing standards or something else called democracy. Democracy was a wonderful thing—it let all sorts of people get as rich as they wanted, and then you found out they were quite nice people after all.

[23]

I may not have put it quite so tidily at the time—but I felt, confusedly, that there was a riddle somewhere. Mr. Shore had made lots of money—he had dug it out of the ground in the magic West. And that was as right as could be, and showed what a nation we were. But Violet shouldn't have worn the sparkling pin to Jane Harvester's party—that wasn't quite nice—and she didn't go to Miss Ainsworth's Dancing Class. I couldn't see that the latter fact bothered her particularly—but the ladies who called on Mother seemed to think it should. But then they were not to be trusted, for they said she was being brought up like a wild Indian, which was obviously absurd, though I wished it were true.

"Of course," Mother would say, with a Latin wave of her hands, "it is hard for me to understand our American distinctions any more. I'm afraid we have drunk too deep of the waters of the *cinquecento*, as a family. But I am very much interested in your great business men. They are doers, and the artist respects the doer. Respects and understands. I cannot help thinking of Pope Julius when I see a man like Mr. Shore . . ."

The callers would generally be quite impressed

by Pope Julius—he was, necessarily, a Romanist, but so far away in time that one could almost forget it. But they would be even more impressed by Mother's understanding Mr. Shore. Somehow, she gave the impression that, if Father had only lived, James Shore would certainly have commissioned him for a Sistine Chapel at least. I don't know quite how she did it, but it was rather clever, for it immediately created a wholly respectable, if entirely imaginary, link between the two families. But I didn't appreciate the cleverness at the time.

She built up for Violet, too, a wholly imaginary character—the lonely, white-faced little princess of a Frances Hodgson Burnett serial, a trifle sickly but wistful and purple-eyed. I knew perfectly well that Violet was as strong as a horse, and yet, basely, I would sometimes give an assenting mutter when Mother spoke gravely of her health. We learn that mutter so early in this world.

As for her loneliness, that seemed to us both a very decided advantage. "What do you do, the days when I don't come up?" I asked her once, with what I did not know was jealousy.

"Oh," she said, "sometimes I play with the other children in the Park. But I don't like them much—

particularly girls. They're so squealy. They make up clubs and giggle." She seemed puzzled that I was interested. "Of course, there's Aleck, but he's not much good at a lot of the things I like," she added, dispassionately. "That's why I like you better. Why don't you come and live with us?" she said.

"Thanks a lot," I said. "But I don't think I could, right away. Besides, I've got to be an artist."

"Oh, you could be that, if you wanted to," she said. "Father wouldn't mind. Oh, well, I suppose they'd make a fuss. They generally do." She dismissed the subject. "Anyhow, we can both of us grow up, and that's one thing," she muttered, under her breath.

"What would you do if you were grown up and had a million dollars?" I said.

"Well," she said, "I guess I will have. But I'll have to go to school, first."

I tried to think of the million, but my imagination wouldn't stretch. "You ought to buy paintings with some of it," I said, earnestly. But I knew I didn't care.

"Maybe I will," she said cheerfully. "But I'll have lots of things to do."

After that we talked over, very thoroughly, the
lives we had each of us lived, so far, and decided
they were interesting but worthless, except in
spots. She could barely remember Gunflint, and
that mostly from Aunt Amy's reminiscences, but
she gave me a feeling of the raw hills, gouged apart
by men for the ore. I had nothing to compete
with that picture, but I did my best. She liked
hearing about Versailles, particularly the foun-
tains.

"If I had them," she said once, "I'd have them
squirt all the time."

"There isn't enough water," I said.

"Oh, that'd be easy," she said. "You could bore
a hole or something. Father could fix it."

So we came to discussing, quite solemnly, the
life we wanted. It wasn't to grow up and be married, it was now, or rather, then, we were going
to be trappers and live in the Rockies. I suppose
most children have had similar dreams at one time
or another, but this wasn't dreaming, it was a life.
We didn't give each other names out of Fenimore
Cooper. It was real, or we made it so, the black
mountains and the wild grass pastures, the blind
snow and the very cold running streams. It used

[27]

to bore Aleck to tears. There wasn't enough fighting in it to suit him. "You and your traps!" he'd
say. "You and your old traps! And then I'm an
Indian and I come along with a gun—bang—
bang . . .""

But we ignored him, we didn't like to play it
that way. Our Indians weren't little lead figures
out of a box—they were real as nightmare and
cruel as the North Wind. We couldn't touch them,
but we knew they were there, at night particularly,
when the thick snow fell on the roof of the cabin
from the overloaded pines. Aleck always had to
touch things before he could feel strong.

Sometimes it seems, looking back, as if it must
have happened—and that it was a just life, even
to the burning death at the end when the Indians
had come indeed. We all have a little of it, I think,
the born Americans—even the city born—the nos-
talgia, the sickness of the frontier. It's a different
curse from Europe's and a different fate. I thought
I was only American by name and rule, but it must
have been in me, too.

It was in James Shore's strength and in Aleck's
strong weakness. Even feckless Aunt Amy had a
touch of it. We all want something for nothing and

[28]

we want it right away. We do not want security but a kingdom. And, when we get it, the fate begins to take hold.

It wasn't the fate that spoiled it for me—it was Mother. She bearded James Shore in his office—it must have been an incredible interview. The next time he looked at me for quite a while, as if he had just met me, and his eyes were tired and guarded.

"Well, Colonel," he said at last, with weary friendliness, "your mother seems to think you're a genius. I suppose we'd better see."

I turned bright red and couldn't say anything. It was too horrible for words. Aleck laughed, and James Shore's brows knotted.

"You needn't, son," he said, with a blighting patience. "I don't know much about it, but I guess it's time we had geniuses. We've got money to pay for them now."

He spoke as if they were coal, to be bought by the ton, but there was a perfect willingness in his voice.

And so I had my audition. I still dream of it at night, even now, and wake up sweating. Because Violet liked me, James Shore got Rinaldo and Streitz to hear me. And I knew what it meant.

[29]

I knew, when I came into the room, that they'd be polite, if they could, to James Shore's *protégé*. They were honest enough, but he was a power. And I had a certain florid knack. I might have been —who knows?—with luck, a *prix de Conservatoire*. You find them in café orchestras, sometimes, still first violins. And they die, and there's a note that they were that. Often, they don't die for a very long time.

I played as well as I could—I was honest enough for that. Afterwards they sent me out of the room with Mother. I had that awful, helpless, childish feeling of things being out of my hands. Then James Shore and Mother talked, and then he said to me, casually, "Well, Colonel—it seems to be all right."

I wasn't happy, that night. I was too excited to sleep, and I kept seeing how it would be. The velvet shorts to make me look even younger and the life led by the hand. It wasn't myself alone, there were Imogen and Enid and Carlo. If it began, it wouldn't stop. We'd climb like Boston ivy, fist over fist. A year before, I would have taken it as my birthright. But since then I had talked with Violet and seen the trains.

[*30*]

Next morning I went alone to James Shore's office. It was one of the few brave things I ever did. Because, after all, it had been Mother's triumph. And I didn't want to go.

I had to get in to see him and I did. And there he was, with his arid friendliness. But I knew what I wanted to say and I managed to say it. And when I began to cry, in the middle, I cried without shame.

I saw why he was James Shore, though, for he believed me instead of trying to comfort me. Indeed, at the end, he said, "Well, Colonel, I appreciate this. Won't you have a handkerchief? I don't know much about these things. But they seemed to think it was all right."

"They'd have said it was all right if I'd been Aleck!" I said, indignantly, and saw, for an instant, a gaunt humor in his face.

"Yes," he said. "I see. It happens a good deal, you know. I'm not like Rudolph. He can tell about things like that. Jews generally can. But I told your mother. I generally do what I tell people."

"Oh," I said, suddenly homesick for the safety of Europe. "If you want to do anything—send us back!"

[*31*]

"If you were a little older, Colonel," he said, suddenly. "But no, it wouldn't work out."

"I want to be a trapper in the Rockies with Violet," I said, and he laughed tolerantly. Even he just took it as the conventional little boy's dream.

"I'm afraid the present fur trade wouldn't offer scope for a man of your abilities, Colonel," he said. "But don't worry. We'll fix something up."

He looked at me again.

"Violet ought to go to school," he stated. "But where will I send her? It's hard figuring these things out. I suppose I ought to get married again, really. But I'm damned if I'll marry a fancy woman. Not after Grindstone City. Well, Colonel, no use bothering you with things like that."

I saw his likeness to Violet extraordinarily, for a moment, though it wasn't anything in the features. And I felt oddly moved. I'd even have been a genius, at the moment, for James Shore. At the same time I could have cried anew because he hadn't understood about the Rockies. He should have understood.

Mother was very angry and excommunicated me sorrowfully from Bohemia. I didn't blame her at all, and I felt that it all was true. And yet, I remember, in the middle of the scene, looking at her and suddenly thinking that I was myself, not any other, and that I would always be myself, no matter what happened. It was one of those queer flashes that sometimes come in a life, and it was mixed with the thought that I mightn't have to wear Fauntleroy suits any more, but it was important. For one can go through years, wearing one coat or another, and only find, in the end, that it never fitted at all.

The excommunication did not last, and, within a week, Mother was planning a future for me as a Medici. But I knew that something was altered nevertheless. I knew it when I saw Violet for the last time. We didn't know it was the last time, for we didn't know she was going to get a cold. I remember running very hard with her down that long mall in the Park where all the bad statues are and hearing Aunt Amy call timidly after us. Violet's hair ribbon came off, and she stuffed it down the neck of her dress impatiently. After that we sat on a bench and ate peanuts and kicked our heels. We were both of us hot from running, and my underwear tickled. It wasn't romantic in the least, and yet as the sparrows began to gather for the peanut crumbs I felt full of an emotion that I did not understand.

We talked again about running away to the West, but we both knew we would not, now. "But I'll send you a postcard, Garry, if Father takes me in the private car," she said, and I nodded. "I'll send you a postcard from France," I said, "with a French stamp."

"Do you suppose you'll be awfully sick?" she asked interestedly. "Aunt Amy's always carsick on trains, and sometimes Aleck is, too. It makes him mad, but he is."

"Well, it takes a pretty good sailor not to be sick, on boats," I said bluffly. "But I guess I'll be all right."

Her hands were stubby and pink, with grime in the lines of the palms. I wanted to do or say something, but I had no terms to express the thing that I felt. I only knew that it hurt me.

"You've got silly-looking hands," I said. But Aunt Amy came up before we had a real chance to quarrel, and that was the end. James Shore was going to take us to the Eden Musée that week, but Violet's cold developed as soon as she got home. So him, too, I did not see again. But all that week

[*34*]

I had dreams about Indians until Mother finally scolded me for waking Carlo up.

When we got on the boat at last, we were all of us glad, even I. Mother was shaking the dust of an ungrateful homeland from her feet, and she did it superlatively. It was exciting, smelling the smells again and hearing the quick, light snarl of French as the sailors cast off the ropes. The others had taken me back as soon as we knew that we were going to sail, and that was comfortable, too. I was part of the clan again, part of the trunks and the memory books and dear Leonardo and all the baggage of those that wilfully carry the torch. But deep in my pasteboard suitcase that didn't look like an American one was a present Violet had given me—an unspeakably ugly glass paperweight with a colored picture of Central Park on the bottom—the sort of thing children buy if they're let alone. And when the last rope was cast off and all the others were yelling, my excitement suddenly died and I felt lonely and naked. For it was then I realized, with almost an adult clarity, that, against my will, I had fallen in love with something, and now, because I had been honest, I was leaving it behind.

PART II

I GOT one smudged letter from her, a month after we landed. And I think I wrote a couple. But Mother was always so anxious that I should write. "My little knight must write to his far-away princess. And I'll be the clever old witch who sends it by a magic—let me see—a magic frog. Hippity hop, Sir Knight, the frog awaits thy missive. Hold your pen a little straighter, dear."

Meanwhile I wouldn't be listening, I'd be trying to remember; and, with each day and each month, relentlessly, the hard edges of New York dissolved and I forgot more and more, till, at last, they all blurred together, Violet's face and the smoke of the trains and the clear, impeccable light of American morning. I would try to remember the look of a certain street, and there would be a cock's-feather officer at the corner instead of a policeman, and the engines of my dreams grew shorter and stubbier, day by day. Time is an adult enemy, and what chance has a child? I don't even remember when the paperweight was lost.

We had the old studio back, now, near the Spanish Steps, and the floor below it, as well, and Mother forgave America after all. For those years were the commencement of the great hegira—the traveling Americans—and wherever a bewildered, newly rich family or a conducted tour wandered over Europe, you began to see almost as many *Jaunty Hearts* as Baedekers, with the corners turned down at the right page. Mother became increasingly regal, in letters to her publishers, and it wasn't any time at all before the autographs began.

It was one of Mother's great times, and she enjoyed it. Somewhere, in an old *Bookman*, there is a photograph of Catherine Grant, the authoress,

with her children grouped about her. Enid and
Imogen are brooding over her shoulders, and
Carlo and I are sprawled picturesquely at her feet.
More picturesquely than comfortably, for our legs
had to be doubled up, to get them out of the way
of the camera, but we all look very original and
talented. Behind us, vaguely, on the wall, is
Father's "Nero Denying Mercy to a Group of
Christians"—or a portion of it, for it was very
large. But you can make out the arena and the
woolly lion and Nero's thumb, on the edge of the
imperial box, turned down as firmly as a sema-
phore. We are all of us looking at Mother, even
the lion, but she is looking straight out toward
fame, and one firm hand lies upon an open book
in her lap. The other rests on Carlo's curls.

It is all artistic, but it is all perfectly respectable,
and on top of the palpably false Venetian chest
are two sweet-grass baskets presented by an
admirer from Maine. Tourists usually found the
studio charmingly foreign and so did Italians,
though not quite in the same way.

And the days went on, and Enid began to go
sketching with her water-color painter under one
of two white umbrellas—they had met in the

English sketch class, and their fate was obvious from the first. His name was Arthur Lakeside, and he had a private income and the mild, uxorious eyes of one born to father a large family. And Imogen settled unwillingly into being Mother's secretary and helping Miss Binks with the dancing class at the Anglo-American School. But I had discovered what I thought was life, at De Vecchi's workshop, and the taste was strong in my mouth. De Vecchi made fakes, but at least he knew what he made and his hands had a passion for good wood. I learned some slang and a good deal about furniture, and I can still remember the rain on Carlotta's window and the rag stuffed into the pane and the senseless pride I felt at being a man.

There is not much to tell about that—we were hungry and ate—and she was perfectly healthy and unscrupulous. I pulled the German courier's nose for him and suffered the jokes of the shop, in the admitted way. Meanwhile I consoled myself with the thought that I intended to be a philosopher and that that was one way to learn. I knew I would never really be a workman, though I liked the feel of gouge and plane in my hand much better than I had the feel of the fiddle bow. But I hadn't the long patience or the roots of instinct, and, as De Vecchi said, I wore too many clean shirts.

With Mother's fame came the healing of the breach with my father's family, and Aunt Alice and Uncle Roger came to Enid's wedding. They came abroad every three years for cultivation and improvement—it was as fixed a ceremony as Uncle Roger's daily cold bath. It was strange to me to see my father's face, indefinably altered yet indefinably the same, above the clerical collar which Uncle Roger wore with grey tweeds on his holiday to show that he was a churchman but broad-minded—to see it repeated again, something about the eyes, something in the poise of the head, above Aunt Alice's boning, the hair strangely grey and a woman's and yet the likeness still. It was, somehow, both uncomfortable and touching.

They helped us a great deal with the Lakesides, and yet they had a disrupting effect upon us. I could see Imogen being drawn to them, slowly and instinctively—and, with that seeing, could recognize why Mother and Imogen had never quite got on. I could see how it all had happened, far back, before any of us were begotten, and what Father had escaped from and why. It must have

[*43*]

been chilly, in Boston, after the Italian sun—
stronger men than my father had found it so, and
he had been the petted child. They had sent him
to Europe to cure a cough—they had not expected
him to become an artist, and the consequences
had appalled them. I was glad I was half an
Antwerp—the Antwerps had made money instead
of being artists, and Mother was still bitter about
Grandfather Antwerp's will. But they had not
bothered as much as the Grants about the Fear of
the Lord. And yet, whenever Uncle Roger spoke
of my father, there was a different expression on
his face, the shadow of something that went back
to boyhood and was still impossible to forget.

When he and Aunt Alice left at last, they took
Imogen with them. "All my chicks are flying away
from me!" sighed Mother, but, on the whole, I am
sure that she was relieved. I think she had rather
dreaded the idea of Imogen's taking care of her in
her old age. It would have been Imogen's turn, then,
to tell her what not to eat. But now, with Imogen
already beginning to do her hair like Aunt Alice,
she could think of her as an Iphigenia, offered up
on the altar of family, and feel very much better
about everything. She wrote "The Empty Nest—

[*44*]

A Wee Sheaf Of Memories" and had quite a gay winter that year.

I had not known it, when Enid and her Arthur departed in a cloud of rice for the journey that was to take them first to the hill towns and then to the house in Surrey—the house with the simple but artistic china and the Japanese prints on the walls. But, when I was shaking hands with Uncle Roger, in the station, and noticing, automatically, that Imogen already looked like any of the American girls whose families were taking them home again, I knew that, sooner or later, there would be a train for me. Yet I kept on with De Vecchi through the winter, for I wanted to know something of selling as well as making. And, also, there was Carlo. We were not particularly emotional with each other—Mother always supplied the emotions —but I thought about him a good deal.

Meanwhile I began to notice that Father's pictures were coming down, one by one, from the walls. So, when Mother finally announced her intentions, I wasn't particularly surprised. Guido was as poor as a church mouse, but the title was real enough, and most of the interesting bits in *A Jaunty Heart in Rome* were his. If he wanted comfort and a bosom to lean on, at bottom he was a very decent little fellow, and his admiration of Mother was entirely genuine. "Your mother," he would say, with his friendly, soft, fox-terrier eyes gleaming, "she is wonderful, your mother! She is a marvel of nature. Ah, how I should like to see your mother beside the Niagara Falls!"

He didn't mean to be funny—they were both acknowledged wonders, and he thought of them in the same breath.

"It'll be all right," said Carlo, when we talked it over. "She'll bully him a good deal, at the beginning, but sometimes he'll bully her, only quite nicely. And that will be good for her and she will like it." He was not very childlike, for a child.

"I can't imagine him bullying anybody very much," I said. "But how about you?"

"Oh, I shall be all right, too," said Carlo. "I like Guido. He has taste. He told me an interesting story, this morning, about his washerwoman. It was well told, very simple. I have already told him that I approve."

"Oh," I said.

"Yes," said Carlo. "I suppose there will be a row, with Enid and Imogen. Though I don't see why there has to be. After all, it is not as if Mother would have any more babies. It will really be very helpful, having Guido in the house. I shall have much more time to think about being an engineer."

"Mother thinks you're going to be another Stevenson," I said. "So you'd better watch out."

"I would rather be the one who built the light-house. That is more solid," said the twelve-year-old. "Oh, you need not worry about me, Garry. I shall take care of myself."

His eyes were round and boyish in his sharp face, but you couldn't help believing him. Even then, even as a child, there was a little core of hardness in him that nothing could melt or taint. All the valuable people I have known have had that core.

Well, he was my chief concern, and, if he was satisfied, I was free. Imogen wrote a long letter, full of quotations from *Hamlet*, and announced that henceforth she considered Uncle Roger and Aunt Alice as her parents—but, as Mother remarked, with one of her occasional flashes of complete common sense, it was rather late to begin that sort of thing and Imogen had always been a Doane. Besides, she misspelt both "Hyperion" and "satyr," and Mother took a good deal of pleasure in pointing it out. Enid did not reply at once, for she was in an interesting condition and, apparently, spent most of her time looking at plaster casts of the Elgin marbles, but Arthur wrote quite sympathetically and offered to illuminate the Capponegri arms, on vellum, for a wedding present. He actually did so, later, and Guido was quite proud of it—it included a genealogical tree growing out of the loins of Æneas, and Guido hung it in his dressing room where he could look at it while he shaved.

And, after Mother's wedding, I went north to Paris and a new life. I walked under the candles of the chestnut trees, and France seemed very clear and reasonable after Italy, and I thought I would make my life there, sanely and deliberately, and rise in it, tooth and nail. I might not carry the torch, and America was a broken glass paperweight, left in another winter, but there were other things. There was still the world, and I had a little money and certain introductions. I played my own hand after them, but they served.

It was the time that never existed—the time before the war—and the hates and treacheries of the Dreyfus case lingered in the white-and-gold salons. I remember going to a house with Dicky de Saugres once, and his whispering to me as we entered, "*Attention, petit! Je flaire l'Affaire.*" He spoke exactly as if he had smelt bad drains, and it was like that, a gaseous, pervading ill. Whatever were men's beliefs, they saw France dishonored. They were glad of any diversion to turn their minds from the shadow of the man on Devil's Island—and I, in my minute way, became one of those diversions. I am not particularly ashamed of it—one always works hard when one is a diversion. Every year, in every city, there are people with new parlor tricks, who appear and vanish. My own was a series of imaginary dialogues, to piano accompaniment, Brünnhilde and Georges Ohnet, Queen Victoria and Oscar Wilde. They sound remarkably dreary in retrospect, and I have no doubt they were so. But they were better than the memory books and the talk about dear Leonardo, for, at least, they were mine.

If you wish to make a place for yourself in any new society, it is always easiest to begin at the top. The bottom knows you by instinct, and the middle is impervious, but there are always a few so sure

of themselves that they do not care who you are
as long as you are new. And, in those days, if you
were an American, you still came from behind the
moon. So I happened to see things and meet people
I might not have seen or met otherwise. I was a
little dazzled by it, I suppose. But I thought myself very logical and Latin. I had youth, a little
money, and a knack of making acquaintances. I
would play them for what they were worth and
see where they led.

They led uphill and downhill and all around
Robin Hood's barn. I have worn dress clothes when
I was actually hungry, and felt a little sick at the
first strong odor of warmth and food and flowers
when the dining-room doors were thrown open and
everyone took such a time to go in. But that did
not last long. For I realized, with a flash of Mother's
occasional common sense, that I must have another life to fall back on, and that, since I was an
American, my new acquaintances would not particularly care what it was, as long as it made no
active demands upon them.

I got in touch with some of the men De Vecchi
had told me about—with Guimard and Krutschler,
the Austrian, and Mannheim, the terrific old Jew

who sweated his painters to the bone and yet bought them, for the price of their poverty, when no one else dared. Whenever one of them died, he was torn between joy and grief. A dead painter was so much easier and more profitable to handle than a living one, and yet he would have to send a bead wreath to the funeral, for there was something in his heart that respected both art and death. I found a shop where he could get most impressive and lugubrious wreaths for a franc and a half less than was his custom, and he let me take two sketches by Zamacoya which I have still. One is a ballet dancer, leaning down to fix her slipper, and the other is a woman who yawns as she washes her hands. They are small and they have few lines, but one is fatigue and the other a sleepy waking, and they will always be that, though we are used to the method now. I wish I had a sketch of Mannheim as well, but he was superstitious about being drawn. There is nothing left of that rapacious vitality but a name for the art critics, and that, too, is just.

Guimard was the most honest of the lot, and, gradually, we got to trust each other, or as far as one can in that world. He was that most immovable of beings, a Parisian of the Parisians, and yet he knew all Europe, by collectors and museums and rivals, and could tell you exactly where the Florentine tapestries hung in some great English house that he had never seen. And he was the first person to give me a sense of the flow of art and treasure with the rise of nations to power and their fall— the inexorable way in which masterpieces drift over mountains and seas, from the strong hand to the stronger, endlessly, to be locked in kings' treasuries, to be shown on walls to the people, but always following the strength and the gold. The currents moved and altered, and Guimard and his fellows watched the currents.

We slipped into a working arrangement; it brought me little money but a great deal of knowledge, and I began to plot the currents for myself. Meanwhile I was also writing a Paris letter, once a week, for one of those solid old-fashioned English newspapers that existed then. Why they wanted a Paris letter at all I never discovered, except that the date line still held a faint and appealing flavor of wickedness—but they continued to print it relentlessly, even at the height of the Boer War. It had to be solid stuff, for the most part, with just the right note of Anglo-Saxon superiority—the evils of absinthe was always good for half a column, but I still remember the communication from the home office that stated, simply and succinctly, when I had referred to Salomé, "We do not feel that Birmingham is interested in modernizations of the Scriptures." Next week I gave them a highly colored account of Sarah Bernhardt's pet tiger cub, and that was all right.

It was a queer, fascinating, improbable life, and perhaps not the best sort of education for the young. But it had its own flavor—the flavor of a world not yet rocked to its foundations, in spite of the drums of maneuver and the hunger of sweated men. There was time to drive in the Bois and worship Satan and write poems about snake charmers and Cynara, to ride bicycles and discuss *le mot juste,* to be interested in coronations and anarchists and balloons and the New Woman. There was such a great deal of time. The gas lamps were not quite blown out, the first flimsy machines had not yet risen into the air. We were all of us eager for the new century, those who were young, but we did not really think of it as changing. The old fools would be put in their places and we would inherit the earth, but life itself would continue, on the fixed rails of Progress, like a more and more splendid train.

As for love, in the world I wished to live in, it was very pleasant but nothing to break the heart. You could be ruined and eaten up by love, but still it was the flesh that suffered the pang. There was the business of capture and the business of betrayal. There were certain phrases and gestures and the mark the high corset left on the naked flesh. Occasionally a fire would roar and devour and people would drop from the world. But, in the main, they departed correctly for the Grand Restaurant of Cythera, to the sound of the first automobile horns, to the roll of the wheels of smart carriages in graveled driveways, those women in lace and petticoats with the high-heeled, pretty shoes and the breasts and voices of pigeons, those men in the English clothes that they never wore like Englishmen, sharp-tongued and witty in a form, killers of game in November with English guns. I can see them before me now, the beards and the mustaches, the wide hats, the last of the fans, but they are already faint. We have eaten one world and are ready to eat another, and the cos-

tumes are in the museums. Nevertheless they lived
when I was young.

And even now, if I shut my eyes, I can see the
lobby of the hotel and the Shores, just arrived in
the dusty clothes of travel, bewildered and tired,
with half a dozen pages fighting for their bags.
They had come some of the way by automobile,
which was still a marvel, and Violet was wearing
the most unbecoming of costumes ever designed
for woman, the long linen duster and hat with a
veil of the early motorists. But she had unpinned
the veil, and I knew her at once. You could not
forget the hardy face or the eyes.

"*Tiens,*" said Dicky de Saugres. "*Voilà des
compatriotes!* She is a very Gibson girl, isn't she?
Regard her virginal aspect and her so rich papa.
La Gibson girl *est toujours vierge, même mariée,
n'est-ce pas? C'est la formule.*"

He was quite proud of his English and I didn't
bother to correct him.

"*Chut!*" I said. "I used to know them. At least,
I think I——"

"*Dans le Far Ouest?*" he said, eagerly.

"*Non, idiot. A New York. Nous étions très
petits, mais——*"

"*Ah*," he said, with a sigh. "*J'aimerais mieux le Far Ouest. L'amour à six ans dans les* wigwams. *Les chercheurs d'or. La petite Fleur de la Prairie.* The papa—is he very rich? He has the air of dollars. *Faut refaire la connaissance, petit!*"

I'd always been amused by Dicky, but I wasn't then.

"No," I said. "I was wrong, after all. They aren't the same people. Come on, let's have a drink."

"How American!" said Dicky, with a devilish grin. "He sees his love of childhood after many years. Does he utter a cry of rapture and bound to clasp her in his arms? No, he says, 'Come on, let's have a drink.' *C'est la vraie morgue britannique, ça. Je suis choqué. Allons.*"

We went, but although we did so, I knew that something had happened. I was making my place, I was very sure of my world. There was no reason on earth why either James Shore or his daughter should even remember my existence. And yet I felt perfectly certain that we would meet.

The occasion happened to be Dicky, but it might have been anything. He came into my room, one morning, before I was up.

[56]

"*Écoutes, farceur!*" he said, shaking me gently. "*Tu me fais une blague, hein?* I have seen the Miss Shore. I have talked with her. She remembers you. Her papa has many dollars. *C'est chic. Elle est adorable, ta* squaw!"

So, some nights later, I sat beside her at dinner, while Dicky chirped and twittered across the table. There were other people as well, chiefly from the American colony. I don't remember the faces or the names, but I could feel the invisible, insistent current of their wishes, focused upon James Shore, as he sat at the head of the table, drinking little and saying less, with his beard very black against his shirtfront and his dark eyes alien and secret as the eyes of a bird. There was a flicker in them when he turned them upon Violet, but that was all. He had changed very little in twelve years, I thought—and yet I knew somehow, suddenly, that I was seeing him at a high point in his life, though I had not been reading the American newspapers and knew nothing of American Copper and the empire all but built. There was a faint tinge of color in his cheeks from the warmth of the room. I wondered what he wanted now, what he could want.

I turned to meet Violet's eyes and forgot about

James Shore. We were shy with each other at first
—she seemed so grown up to me now—but that
passed. I can't even remember what we said.
Except that once she looked at me and said,
"We're here. I've always wanted to be here," and
there was youth and a victory in her voice. After
dinner we sat through an interminable blank-verse
tragedy, which James Shore suffered, as he suffered
so many things, with his dusty patience. And then,
going back in the carriage, Violet and I were next
each other again and I could feel her shoulder
against mine. That was all that happened, but it
was the crest of a wave. I felt as if we must drive
forever, to the clop of the horse's hoofs, through
the chilly streets of spring. It was not even love, it
was something we should always keep. Then, next
morning, I waked and remembered who we were.

But as soon as I'd had coffee I went down to the
hotel, and on the way I stopped at a flower stall
and bought a great many primroses. They sold
them in big bunches then, for a franc or so, though
I forget how much I paid. The woman was young,
and she overcharged me and wished me luck with
my girl, and I felt oddly grateful, oddly shy.

So I became what was inevitable, the nameless

friend of the family, the unpaid courier. I knew
what my French friends thought; they were real-
ists. I knew what Dicky de Saugres thought, for he
let me know, with infinite delicacy and cynicism,
exactly what price might be expected for my active
aid. It began with a slightly mustached fourth
cousin of the De Saugres who had no *dot* but was,
he assured me earnestly, "the most boring and ad-
mirable of *jeunes filles*," and ended with a percent-
age on the furnishings of the pink marble house he
intended to build on the Avenue du Bois, when he
married Violet. For, by then, James Shore's name
was known and the flies were at the honeypot.
They were a trifle less blatant, then, a trifle more
subtle. But they came.

And through it all moved Violet, walking so
firmly. That face, so fresh in Europe, that face
which is like coming home.

We talked about Roberts and the train, we
talked about other things. We felt very adult,
talking, though a lot of it was at cross purposes at
first. For most of what had been her life since I
last saw her, I didn't know. The names, except for
one or two, like the Harvesters, meant nothing to
me. But I felt there had been a struggle and a

[*59*]

change. I remember her saying, when we'd both laughed over some memory, "It was fun. But I didn't know."

"Didn't know what?" I said.

She stirred in the little gilt chair. "Oh," she said, "lots of things. I'm still a barbarian, Garry. Every now and then I feel like one. New York's pretty snobbish. A lot of fat old ladies, sitting around. Father doesn't pay attention to things like that. He wouldn't. So I had to do it. It probably all sounds silly to a man. Being asked the right places and all that. But I guess it is important. It seems to be."

Her face looked a little puzzled at some interior thought.

"I wonder what Mother was like," she said. "Aunt Amy's told me a lot, but you know Aunt Amy. And then she cries. I'd like to really know. She was a school teacher, and I remember how pretty her hands were. I think we must be quite different. Father called one of the shafts the Mary Shore. She didn't want to come to New York, but she came. It's all happened so quickly, Garry."

We were sitting in one of those palm corners that existed in ballrooms then, and she struck her fan on her knee. The light thing made a sound, and she looked at it.

"Old women, telling you what to do," she said. "I'd like to tell them what to do."

"You will," I said, and I meant it, though at times I was amused. But not that time.

One by one the skins of Europe sloughed from me. I did not even think of her as herself—inexperienced, for all the panoply of the Gibson girl, and often very much alone, I thought of her as something triumphant—a conquering goddess— the Liberty of the old half-dollars, youthful and a little stern. Behind her were the magic names and the new incantations, the names of the great stocks and the great railroads, the White Fleet, cruising the oceans, and the full sweep of the land. It made me feel both humble and curious. Even Aunt Amy's woolwork took on a borrowed splendor, and I studied the novels of Richard Harding Davis as I would have studied textbooks. They filled me with hopeless envy—surely life could not be quite so simple as that, even for born Americans. But it must be so, for Violet said it was.

"Oh, of course there are slums and things," said Violet. "We had a course in civics at Miss Bailey's.

But you can't help that. We're the melting pot of the world."

"The melting pot," I said. I could hear it bubbling, a vast caldron of metals—of gold and iron and fudge and college pennants and men—to be cast into new astonishing shapes that were like no shapes before.

"Yes," said Violet. "I tried to explain it to your friend Dicky de Saugres, but I don't think he understood, though he was very polite."

"I'm afraid he wouldn't," I said, seeing the scene. "The French don't like the idea of being melted. Except when it's somebody else."

"Yes," said Violet, unexpectedly. "I'm not a child, Garry. I know it's different. But I wanted to come." She moved restlessly. "I slapped a girl's face once, at school, for saying Mother was a washwoman," she said. "But that was all right, because one of the teachers heard her, and they took her away next term and put her in a college. She was a Chicago girl, with big ears. Her father wasn't very much, anyway. Just dry goods. But somebody made them a pedigree showing they were descended from Edward the Confessor, and she thought she could be proud."

"But Edward the Confessor didn't have any descendants," I said.

"Then they got the wrong pedigree," said Violet, placidly. "Or perhaps it was a joke of the man's. They wanted to sell Father one showing we were descended from Charlemagne, but he said it took in too much territory. Aunt Amy liked it, though. It had dozens of coats of arms." She laughed a little. "They have to be real, don't they?" she said with a smile.

"Well," I said, feeling very broad-minded, "Dicky's is real enough."

"Yes," she said. "He's a nice little man." She moved again. "It's fun, being here," she said. "But it makes you feel old, too. With everything so old. You're used to it, aren't you, Garry? I remember thinking how much you knew. But I never told you so."

"You certainly never did," I said, and we laughed again.

"You'll have to tell me a great deal," she said, after a moment, in her spacious voice.

I was used to women who knew and acknowledged their sex as a charm or a treasure or a weapon, but who never forgot it while they lived.

[63]

Beside them she seemed like a new spear. I had grown up early and shrewdly, and a little grimily—it was wonderful to be merely young—to pretend I was one of the magic people just out of a college, with that nice, fresh, puppy-like warmth on their healthy, uncumbered faces, to try and imitate the things they might presumably say. For I knew about colleges, now—hadn't Violet told me about them? Aleck had been to a college and succeeded very well. He had rowed a boat. In a month or so he would be joining the Shores. I thought she was as glad to have him away for a while—I gathered he was something of a responsibility, in spite of having rowed a boat.

"*Tu ne refais pas une connaissance, petit, tu cherches à refaire ta virginité*," said Dicky, acutely, one day. Well, it wasn't exactly that, but there was truth in the phrase. It can happen a great many ways—I have seen it happen in many. It can also happen like that. Because it did happen, and I would not have expected it. I wonder what James Shore thought. But you seldom knew what he thought until he translated it into act. I know he looked at me with a dim smile when I first started wearing American collars, and I felt

[*64*]

abashed because I had not known that he noticed things like that.

Then I met Violet and forgot. We happened to be discussing Aunt Amy, for some reason—perhaps we were waiting for her. At any rate, I remember her saying, "Aunt Amy used to be a very good dancer, you know. They used to dance all night, when they had a house-raising. That was when she was a girl. She was very proud of her slippers because they came from the East, and she cried when the last pair wore out."

I waited, hoping for more, but no more came. She sighed.

"Now it's nothing but waltz and two-step and the lancers," she said. "The men used to come miles in their boots—Aunt Amy's seen them. Of course, it wasn't like anything here," she added, dutifully. "But it must have been exciting." Something gleamed in her eyes.

"I wish I'd been there," she said, "when Father first got the Lucky Dollar. Of course, once he had it, he had to go on. But I wish I'd been there at the start. They fought him, of course," she said, as if to herself. "But then it doesn't matter so much, if people are nice to you. It matters whether you're somebody or not."

Then Aunt Amy came at last, and we went to see a museum, though I cannot remember which. But Violet's words stayed in my mind—for she had looked like a young, indignant Brünnhilde as she spoke them—and they seemed to me a call, a challenge. My cylindrical hat had eight reflections, and I could talk the day's gossip with Dicky and Dicky's friends—but were these occupations for a man? A man should be civilizing Little Brown Brothers on the far-flung outposts of Empire or learning to play the great game of mills and mines and factories—the game of the splendid pirates whose private cars were their palaces, insubstantial as the tents of nomad emperors and, like them, always in motion. They must know, for they had the power—they must be right, for they lived with such imperial disregard for comfort at the greatest possible expense.

James Shore had a special messenger to bring his cables and a room down the corridor fitted up as an office, even to the cuspidors and the roll-top desk— but there wasn't a chair anywhere in the suite it-self that you really liked to sit on, though many of them had gilded Sphinxes for feet. And I have seen him genuinely mortified only once, when he told me of how the hotel valet attempted to dress him. "But there the man was, holding out my own pants. It doesn't seem right, somehow, to have a grown man dress you. Of course, I keep Robert, but that's a different thing."

He looked at me with the slight curve of the lips that was his humor.

"It would have served him right," he said, "if I'd tried to jump into them from a standing start. But I guess it wouldn't have been fair. Well, Colonel, what do you think of the market today?"

I told him, perfectly seriously, that rails seemed a little shaky to me, and he nodded. It had become a fiction between us, I don't know how, that I was an authority on rails but remarkably chary of my inside information. Sometimes I felt half convinced of it myself; he spoke of my commitments with such unwinking gravity. And, always, there were the real telegrams, coming in and going out. I suppose I could have made real money out of them if I had wanted to pry. But you are either born with that gift or without it. Instead I got merely a sense of humming power and battles waged in a mist.

Three telegrams out of four he would read and

throw away unanswered—the fourth he might reply to, generally in four or five words. I remember helping him look up code words for a somewhat longer telegram once, when he was tired. It was all Greek to me, even before it was coded, but, when we'd finished, he sighed a little and said, "Well, that puts McCuan out of business. I've been gunning for him a long time, but now that he's done with, I almost miss the man." I had no idea who McCuan was, but I suddenly saw a woodchuck that had come out once too often and the hunter casually turning the plump body over with his foot, a little regretful now that the long patience was done.

"McCuan?" I said. "Why were you gunning for him?"

"Oh, he thought he had me in a corner about six years ago," said James Shore. "But, as things turned out, he didn't. You know, Colonel, a man like that is a good deal of a nuisance. If you haven't got chips, there's no point sitting in the game."

I was to remember that later and not to my content. But, at the time, I merely put it down in the mental notebook I was keeping under, "Titans: how to become one." I was so sure that I was the

[68]

detached observer and that my observation would never get in the way of my life.

For it all mixed, for a little while, during those first weeks, the reality and the dream. It was really a very short time, but it seemed much longer. I didn't know where time was going and I didn't care. The Shores wanted a guide to Paris—very well, I would be that guide and still keep my integrity, for I asked nothing of them. And Violet and I had decided that we were friends, American friends.

We went to museums and looked at things in glass cases and painted things upon walls. We went to the Exposition and walked in the Rue des Nations, we drank Jordan water at the Petit Restaurant de Jerusalem, we gaped at the weary savages in the native village and the smooth, quiet dynamos, at the tall Russians, walking the streets in clothes too heavy for May and the huge electric star above the Palais de l'Électricité. It was there—the house of the bourgeois—the house of Progress—the house of the solid meals and the safe, eight-per-cent. investments and the little, exciting wars in far corners of the map. It was there, with its looms and its iron and its treasure, with its frock-coated bankers and its plaster horns of plenty—the triumph of the long century—and I walked in it with Violet, recovering the youth I had thought gone by.

I talk as if we were alone, enclosed in a crystal. And now and then, at odd moments, I would have that feeling. But, of course, we were nothing of the kind. Sometimes I wouldn't see her for days, and always there was the crowd of suitors and clients and callers and all the people with things they wanted to sell James Shore.

And then Charles Whipley Morton came over, with Aleck, and he was the genuine article. He knew so well the things I tried to pretend. The two youths had been classmates at college, and there was a fatal likeness that drew James Shore.

It was one step farther, you see, and something James Shore couldn't buy. The portraits were real, in the house at Morton's Hook, and they called their Newport place "The Barn." Charles Whipley was the fourth generation, and he looked like an eldest son.

He was big, and he had such clean teeth and good manners and well-brushed hair. He looked like our best, you know—the young prince who can stand the strain. When he threw back his head to laugh, you thought of a fine, well-tended horse.

Nor was he merely another Aleck. In fact, Aleck's obvious admiration for him was one of the most natural and likable things I ever found in Alexander Shore. It was the simple, physical worship of a schoolboy for a school hero. Aleck copied Charles Morton's ties and his way of talking —he yearned in all men's eyes to be like Charles Morton—he prodded Violet and his father continually to make sure that they fully appreciated this wonderful friend. And James Shore looked on, with his dry, slight smile, and Violet rather enjoyed herself, teasing Aleck about him. I didn't realize it was all a predestined comedy. I even felt sorry for Charles Morton for a while.

He was easy to like, even easy to admire, for, though he had absolutely no humor about himself, he possessed a great deal of charm. It was the kind of thing that makes any boarding school easy for its possessor, though I'm sure that he never thought of it in those terms—charm was something that women had. And with it he had the gift of making you feel, when you were with him, that you were important to him. Though, under-

[*71*]

neath all the physical ease and the impulsiveness of youth, there was a curious, ingrained rigidness —the rigidness which is bred into people of his sort for a defense.

We had as little in common as any two people can have. And yet I spent time I should have given Guimard, discussing himself and his problems and his money with him. It made Aleck jealous, for one thing, and I rather enjoyed annoying Aleck. I listened to manly, incredible confidences—there had been adventures with chorus girls, but Charles Morton was done with that. He obviously thought me very corrupt—I must be, living in Europe all my life—but it was I who was shocked. There was neither glamour nor heat in that recital—not even wit or grace—only mechanism and a haunted fear of publicity. One of the girls had tried to make a fuss and see him, but they'd soon settled that. I'd understand how it was. I didn't, for all my corruption, but I tried to learn.

Demagogues, like Theodore Roosevelt, might betray their own class for a mess of political reform, but money was a huge responsibility. James Shore was a great man, but he didn't quite realize that. The Mortons did, and the future was in their hands, sound and safe as a bond in a safe-deposit box. That was one reason you married early, if you were a Morton. I listened and nodded. Every now and then I'd make a suggestion and he'd say, "Gee, that's great! I'll have to write that to Father." He seemed to have a great respect for his father—and I could see the likeness in the picture he showed me—the picture of that distinguished elder horse.

At times I felt quite intoxicated with power, a Mazarin pulling wires behind the scenes. He seemed so youthful and malleable—there seemed to be so much he wanted to know. When he remarked, earnestly, that he believed in marrying whom you wanted and had often told his father so, I granted him courage and independence and cheered him on. For, after all, James Shore was James Shore, but the Mortons were the Mortons—I had become a little infected with his own attitude by now. Not sufficiently so that I could not laugh at him, now and then, with Violet, though we were always serious in the end.

"He's what Aleck tries awfully hard to be, isn't he?" said Violet, with one of her flashes. "Only, somehow, you feel Aleck trying."

It was a devastating comment, but a true one.

"Well," I said, with a queer pang, "he seems to be giving Aleck a great deal of his priceless time."

"Why, Garry, you really sound jealous!" she said, in an amused voice. "Anyhow, he's leaving for England the end of the month," she said, and I felt relieved. There could be no jealousy between us; we were too good friends for that.

I resolved to be even more forthright and idealistic than usual, and I soon had the opportunity. For the very next time we were with her together, he turned to me, when she had gone, and said, "Look here, old man, she's a wonderful girl and we know it. Let's shake hands."

I did so, feeling much moved.

He looked at his hand as if it had done him a favor.

"That's the way it ought to be between decent people," he said. "A square scrap and no hard feelings. I won't forget it, Grant."

It didn't occur to me, at the time, that under no circumstances could the scrap ever be square. I thought of Dicky and the only English proverb he ever quoted, "All's fair in love and war," and felt very superior. Dicky would never have understood.

And he did not understand. He was frankly and blasphemously puzzled by the whole affair. For James Shore, when he got to know him, he had an odd respect—"*c'est un Peau-Rouge—un vrai Peau-Rouge—mais c'est un homme*"—but Morton and he disliked each other instinctively from the first. He used to call him "*le grand bébé rose*" and ask me solicitously about the state of his *culottes*. And Morton would make heavy jokes about Count No-Rocks to Aleck—college-boy jokes as blunt as the blade of an oar. As for me, I found Dicky's eyes resting upon me in an increasing bewilderment. He couldn't seem to decide whether I was Morton's enemy or his ally or a curiously American combination of both.

Yes, I thought myself very civilized, as the knot drew tighter and tighter. I even had an appalling interview with Madame de Fronjac. She was Dicky's great-aunt and one of those terrifying old ladies one is apt to find embedded in the very core of the French family—old ladies who grow into legend and tyranny with the years. I had heard about Tante 'Line ever since I knew Dicky—I had even been introduced to her—but she had never deigned to notice my existence before.

Now, however, she desired to pump me, and I
could not but admire the spirit in which she did it.
I was brought before her like an orange on a plate,
and she meant to show me exactly the considera-
tion she would have shown to the orange. She would
peel and quarter me with neither waste nor hum-
bug but with a remorseless neatness. And, in the
process, she allowed herself that glacial frankness
which is the prerogative of those who no longer
care what anybody but themselves may say.

We had not been talking five minutes before she
let me know that she considered Dicky an amiable
nincompoop, less stupid than his sisters, certainly,
for it was impossible to be more stupid than they
were, but, on the whole, definitely worthless,
though not without a certain amount of *esprit*.
Nevertheless, as the last male De Saugres, Dicky
had obvious responsibilities, and, for once in his
life, in pursuing Violet, he seemed to be paying
attention to them. As for Violet herself, she had a
large chin and an overripe peasant color, but she
looked as if she would bear healthy children and,
for so tall a girl, did not carry herself too ill.

The priests would settle the religion, and one did
not expect either manners or family from Ameri-

cans. But the crux of the matter was the actual money—one heard a great deal about American wealth, but one had heard the same stories about other nations before. "*Il y avait cette Polonaise,*" she said, darkly, while her eyes remembered a history. "*Oh, oui, oui—elle disait 'mon cousin' à tous les grand ducs—et même ses joyaux étaient faux. Heureusement, elle mangeait comme une carpe et mourait d'une attaque d'apoplexie à l'âge de vingt-trois ans, sans issu. Il se remaria, lui, en 1767— mais c'était très ennuyeux pour la famille.*"

It had happened more than a century ago, but she still took the Polish beauty who had tempted a De Saugres into marriage with her languor and her false jewels as a personal affront. I had been annoyed and then angry, but now I was beginning to enjoy myself.

"*Tu, felix Austria, nube,*" I said, giving the Latin the French sound.

"*Ah—ah—ah—*" she said, on three light, ascending notes of scorn—I will translate the rest for clarity's sake—"Monsieur is well-acquainted with his classics. My nephew has often spoken to me of the talents of Monsieur Grant. Nevertheless——" and she returned to the charge and we fenced till,

[77]

suddenly, I was tired of fencing. I hadn't thought I was showing it but she saw it at once. She gave me a quick glance.

"*Ah*," she said, in the tone of one who discovers an unexpected but interesting difficulty, "but, really, Dicky is too naïf. He did not tell me that."

"Madame—" I said, and felt myself, to my horror, turning red.

She lay back in her chair for a moment, and her eyes were bright with malice and enjoyment and the terrible knowledge of the flesh that sometimes comes to the old.

"Ah, no," she said, putting her hands in repose upon her lap, "he did not tell me that."

"Madame is being pleasant," I said. "Naturally."

"Oh, naturally, naturally," she said, with a sudden violence. "Do you think I cannot find that natural? When I was young——"

"Madame was almost as lovely as she is now," I said, recovering myself.

"No," she said, with an arrogant firmness. "I was never lovely. Extremely pretty—that is all."

We talked for another five minutes on indifferent subjects, and then she signified to me that the audience was terminated. I was glad, for I, too, was beginning to be afraid of her—there was too much knowledge in her eyes. She had tasted all and survived all, and, in the end, there was nothing that could not be tasted or survived. And yet my flesh revolted against that clarity.

When I made my good-byes, she looked at me again.

"And you, too, you are sufficiently naïve, Monsieur Grant," she said, tapping gently on the chair arm. "But perhaps you are right. The naïve are the truly happy. Only—it is difficult to remain so, all one's life."

I bowed over her hand and left her, but I could feel her cold, compelling smile, like an icicle between my shoulderblades, all the way down the winding, carpeted stair. Dicky was waiting for me at the bottom. He gave one look at my face and took my arm.

"*Tu es froissé*," he said, in a low voice, with an uneasy glance up the stair. "*Mon pauvre petit, je te demande mille pardons. C'est ridicule. Elle est la fée Carabosse. Mais, dans la famille, tu sais——*"

You couldn't be angry with Dicky for long and, soon enough, I found myself laughing helplessly

[79]

at his description of a week-end the Shores had spent at Aubenel. "*Mon petit*," he said earnestly, "one has actually picnicked in the *parc* to do honor to American customs. You cannot imagine the effect. Madame, my cousin, de la Chézy found the prettiest little serpent in the grass beside her. It gave her a *crise de nerfs* that nearly strangled her in her own sandwich. And everyone, even Papa, was horribly bited by gnats. All the same, Papa was very pleased with Monsieur Shore. *Au moins, il lui a montré le pigeonnier, les écuries, les portraits, l'épée de mon bis-aïeul et le jupon de Marie Antoinette*," he added, cynically. I waited for the inevitable phrase, and it came. "*Pauvre papa, il est vraiment un peu naïf*," said Dicky de Saugres.

I laughed, but beneath the laughter there was something I did not recognize. The old woman had cracked a glass bubble, and I wanted to see Violet desperately. But, when I did, the next day, we went to the Carnavalet, her father and she and I, and looked at queens' shoes and talked about history. It seemed to me, suddenly, that we were all on a strain, and I wondered if the Shores had been in Europe too long. Then we went back to the hotel and up to the suite. I didn't intend to go, for I had an appointment with Guimard, but Violet wanted to show me some snapshots. She took off her hat, like a schoolgirl, as soon as she got in the sitting room—she always hated hats, and I remember her drawing the long pins out of this one and shaking her head with relief. There was a little heap of letters and telegrams for James Shore on the table, and I saw his eyes stray to it.

"Will you and the Colonel excuse me for a few minutes?" he said. "I want to get off early to that Chartres place, tomorrow, if we can. I guess your aunt's lying down."

He nodded to us both and went off down the corridor to the room where he had his office. And suddenly, when he was gone, it was like the Sixty-second Street house, for Violet opened Aunt Amy's door and found the room empty and said, "Oh, my, she'll be lost if she's gone out alone. No, she's got her conversation manual," and we both giggled.

She swung her hat in her hand for a minute, as no French girl would have done.

"Now where are those snaps?" she said. "I did want to show you."

[*81*]

"Can't I get them?" I said.

"No, they must be in my room," she said. "Wait a minute, Garry. Oh, dear, I sound just like Father. Or did I leave them with Aunt Amy? Look on my dressing table, will you, Garry, while I look in here—it's silly you shouldn't, and it'll take hours to get the maid."

I had seen girls' rooms before, but not like this one. They'd been living in the suite three months, but there was so little that told of their presence, except for the click of the telegraph down the corridor and James Shore's cigar box and a book called *Daily Seeds For Daily Needs* that Aunt Amy kept on her dresser. The guidebooks and the Tauchnitz novels might have been anybody's, and, while packages were always arriving, they never seemed to contain anything but clothes for Violet and the souvenirs that all tourists buy.

Violet's room was particularly and expensively hideous in a sort of bastard *Art-Nouveau*. But there, on the dressing table, whose legs were wrought-iron carnations, beyond the enormous, silver-backed brushes and combs were her possessions: four photographs, one of her mother, quite dim and yellow; a pair of small china cats with pink bows at their necks; a dusty-looking nugget that must have come from the mine; and an old-fashioned penny with a blue ribbon through it. I don't know why they suddenly struck me as desolate. But, while I rummaged gingerly for the photographs, I felt sad.

I heard her voice from the other room, "All right, Garry, I've found them," and the glass bubble broke. I knew that I loved her then and that I would always love her. It was nothing we had done or left undone, but it had happened. I had fought a long time against it, pretending to be civilized, but that was at an end.

I went back into the room, and we sat on the sofa and looked at the snapshots. I kept thinking that it might have been like this if we had both grown up in Gunflint, if she had been the daughter of one of the mine superintendents and I the school teacher's son. She would have on a cheaper dress, and the dry wind would flap the screen door on the sunburnt porch of summer, but James Shore would still be as secret and she the desire of the eyes. The photographs would be in an album with a burnt-leather cover. I would have done that myself and written her name in purple ink on the page. We would none of us have to change much, even Mother. I wondered for the first time if we had done well to change.

The photographs themselves were like all tourists' photographs of famous scenes, but she seemed very proud of them, and again I felt that sorrow.

"They're so easy to take," she said. "You do just push the button. Of course, it isn't like painting," she added. "But I bet I could do it if I had to. There aren't any women photographers, but that's no reason there shouldn't be. You know Father was a photographer, once."

"Honestly?" I said. It was hard to imagine James Shore saying, "Look pleasant, please."

"Oh, yes," she said. "When he ran away from his father. He went all over the country. They called them tintypes, then. Aunt Amy doesn't like to have him tell about it."

She dismissed the subject. "I wish I had some chocolate cake," she said. "And a cold glass of milk."

"Well," I said, "when Miss Flower comes back, you might both come out to tea with me." But she shook her head.

"No, thank you, Garry," she said. "You're nice

to think of it. But I don't want those funny little tarts and all the waiters saying '*Monsieur—Madame.*' I want a big piece of chocolate cake and *cold* milk. It never gets really cold here, no matter what you tell them.''

She rose and moved restlessly about the room.

"I don't know what's the matter with me," she said. "I guess it's being over here. It upsets me, somehow. Everything's different. There was a bad woman in Gunflint, but everybody knew she was bad. 'She lived unrespected but handsome and died with her boots on.' That's what they used to say. But if I told it to Dicky, he'd be awfully shocked. And yet everybody has—mistresses here —haven't they—even people like Charles?''

I felt remarkably uncomfortable, remembering Charles Morton's handshake.

"If that's part of the course in civics——" I began, rather angrily, but was stopped by the trouble in her face.

"Oh, Garry," she said. "Don't you see I want to talk to somebody? I can't, to Aunt Amy or Aleck, and, after all, Father's older. We've joked about Charles and Aleck. But Charles is going to ask me to marry him, now.''

[*85*]

"I'm sure I wish you the very greatest happiness," I said, stiffly, and got up.

"Oh, *please* Garry," she said. "It isn't settled. He's gone to England, and his father's coming over. We wouldn't be engaged till he came, really. But he—he was rather sweet. He told me about the bad things he'd done and how we weren't going to be like most people. You see, we both have money, so we needn't be afraid of each other at all. You don't know what that's like, especially if you're a girl. He talked as if we'd have children. I can't imagine it, Garry—having a child."

"*Et patati et patata*," I said. "It must have been a touching interview." The words came out of my mouth quite neatly and in sequence, but I could not remember thinking them, only that a glass bubble was broken. "Did he put his head in your lap?" I said. I could see it there.

She drew in her breath, and again her eyes were James Shore's.

"Garry—you're impossible," she said.

"Oh, no," I said. "I'm in love with you. That's the catch. I won't talk to you about children, and there's no way we can get married. But I'm in love with you. Do you know what it's like, being in love? *Gran' Dieu*, it isn't putting your head in somebody's lap and crying!"

"He didn't. He didn't. You're stupid. Stupid and mean."

I took her wrists, and she wrenched at them, and we stared at each other for a moment like angry children. Then I was kissing her, quickly and fumblingly and not as I'd ever kissed woman. Even Dicky would have done it better. There was a queer quietness to it. Neither of us said a word.

Then I looked at her face and saw how she was shaken. There was confusion in it, and amazement and a struggle. "Oh, it isn't fair," she said. "It isn't fair, over here. Why couldn't you have been my brother instead of Aleck? Then everything would be all right."

"Oh," I said. "For God's sake, Violet——"

I saw the vast stupid bed and the silver-backed brushes. So she would brush her hair, in front of the glass. And so Charles Morton would watch her, feeling ashamed but pure. I was not Charles Morton, and I wanted other things.

"Maybe I love you, Garry," she said, in a low voice, and I felt incredible joy. But I also wished to be noble—to play the game in the terms I barely knew.

"You've got to be sure," I said, trembling. "You've got to be very sure."

"Yes," she said, with a queer docility, "I guess I have."

All the same, I took her into my arms again, like wheat and corn, and as I held her, for a moment, I felt it beating, the strong engine of her heart. It beat without flurry or violence, though it beat fast. I kissed her and let her go.

"I don't apologize, and I'm not sorry," I said. "But I'll play fair. Be as free as you choose. I just want a chance to show you." My voice rang in my ears like Rudolf Rassendyl's—I was almost sorry Charles Morton could not see me. And yet, with it all, I felt both the desire of the flesh and the desire of the spirit—and both were strong. I had known the one before but not the other, and it is a lasting thing.

"You're a fine person, Garry," she said. "I'll always know you're a fine person. And I do trust you."

I laughed, a little unsteadily. "I'll try to be worth that," I said, and we looked at each other, solemnly. I think we both felt very proud. I know I did, for I had not behaved like a scoundrel. A scoundrel would merely have tried to win her, without thought of anything else.

I thought I knew so much about women, and when I walked home that evening the pride was still in my mind. I had told her the truth, and next day I would talk to James Shore. It was all very clean and forthright and according to the books. The hero fell in love with the beautiful Miss Van Bibber, but it all came right in the end. I hadn't even pressed her about Charles Morton, though I had wished to, keenly enough. But we hadn't had time, for one thing—Aunt Amy had returned and we had had to pretend. As it was, she had been fussily disturbed at finding us together without James Shore.

It was even lucky, I thought, that James Shore and I were going to Chartres without Violet. It fitted in with the legend, even to the early train and my fevered attempts to put him at his ease. He seemed a little surprised by the attempts, and I hastily decided not to force the issue. So, all the morning, with a new and curious timidity upon me, I showed him around like a guide, talking

[*89*]

about mediæval glass while he listened. After lunch he said, "I think I'll go back to that church, Colonel. Don't bother if you don't want," and I left him alone. I found him, three hours later, staring at the blue window. I'd been sitting in front of a café, in a dream of youth and triumph— I hadn't noticed how quickly the time had passed. Going back in the train he said, "It took a lot of time and a lot of men. But it must have been a great satisfaction."

I said something about the Pyramids.

"I suppose we'll see them," he said. "But that's different. You could live in this town like anybody else and still the church would be there. It isn't just something you go to look at, it's still going on. Even when there's nobody in it. I could build a church, if I wanted, and do it a lot quicker. But how do I know what would happen? Well, Colonel, have a cigar."

I took it, though I didn't want it, and we sat for a moment in silence. Then he smiled his faint smile.

"Want to talk to me about Violet, I suppose," he said.

"Yes," I said and plunged in. I could hear my

voice in my ears, being oratorical, being noble, being fervent. It sounded strange and empty, snatched away by the wind and the wheels and scattered to the flat French landscape, scattered to the dusty poplars and the broad, well-tended fields. I could feel the taste of dust in my teeth as I spoke, and now and then the roar would drown out my words. James Shore had on a flat linen traveling cap that made him look oddly quizzical, and once I saw him reading the name of a station as we passed it. It was not what I had planned. And, all the time, something at the back of my mind kept telling me that it was already settled, in spite of honor and truth and Richard Harding Davis, and that my only chance would have been to steal her away.

When I had quite finished, James Shore looked at his cigar. "Your sentiments do credit to your delicacy, Colonel," he said, rather quaintly. "But, you see, you haven't got chips, and that's a fact."

He held up his hand as I started to interrupt. "Wait," he said, and for a moment both his dustiness and his patience fell from him, and I could see the essential quality in him—the quality that had torn the metal from the hills.

"She's to have the best that's going," he said. "They both are. There's no argument about that."

"I realize——" I said. "I know how——"

"Oh, it's nothing personal, Colonel," he said, relaxing. "But you've got to think about things. I don't know if you ever did farmwork. I did from the time I was five till I went away. My father treated me like a hired hand, except he couldn't lick the hired hand. And it seemed as though the grasshoppers came every year. Aleck's had it pretty easy, but what are you going to do?"

"I do assure you——" I said, but he didn't seem to hear me. He was staring across the landscape, and, as he looked, I could see the trim lines dissolve and the raw earth rise, the back-breaking earth, the treeless swell of the prairie, with nothing between the plow and the sunset but the birds.

"I'll be very frank with you, Colonel," he said, in a slow voice, "Violet thinks a lot of you. And you've been a great help to all of us, over here. Not that I've got anything against foreigners. But they've got different rules than we have, especially about marrying. But you're not a foreigner—and still you know most of the rules.

[*92*]

Now I've had your friend, De Saugres, on my mind for a while."

"Why, what's the matter with De Saugres?" I said.

"There isn't a thing the matter with him," said James Shore, dryly. "He's not like that Prince fellow with the whiskers—I had him looked up, too," he said, and I winced. "But I just imagine he'd be quite a serious investment, if anyone decided to bank on him. You wouldn't deny that, Colonel?"

"No," I said. "I won't deny that."

"Well, there you are," said James Shore. "I'm rather glad you were here when Violet met him and the others. It took a little of the shine off," and he smiled.

It was his entire composure that made me feel desperate.

"That's all very interesting," I said. "But if Violet thinks a lot of me, I think you owe me a chance. I don't say I could ever get as far in the world as you have. But I've got some brains, and I could learn about business, if that's what you want for Violet. Just tell me how to start."

He looked me up and down from beneath his cap.

"You know, Colonel," he said, rather amusedly, "there's one thing about you. You may not have chips. But, for a polite sort of man, you've got a good deal of nerve."

So we made our little treaty. It was quite like the books and not particularly bad. I could give up Guimard and my odd jobs and spend two months in Germany and northern France, looking at certain plants and seeing how they were run. He didn't expect me to understand the techniques, but he wanted to see what I made of the life. "Get hired and fired," he said. "They're both easy, when you're young. And, when you come back, tell me what you make of it. I won't pay you one red cent, but I'll get you a couple of letters, and if you can tell me something I don't know——"

He left the reward in the air, but I knew they always did that. And, as for Violet, hadn't I sworn to play fair? The one unbearable thing would be playing fair, with a crowd of suitors around her. Besides, they'd be traveling, in England mostly, for the rest of the summer. I couldn't follow them there, if I meant to work for my goddess. There was Charles Morton, but I now undervalued

Charles Morton. He was a great, rosy, honorable baby, and I, I felt, was a man.

It was all very sane and sound, and I explained it to Violet. "But I'll miss you, Garry," she said.

"My God!" I said. "Don't you think I'll miss you?" My hands wanted to go to her, but I honorably kept them back.

"I'll miss you," she repeated, childishly. "I did when you went away before."

"Listen," I said, and this time I did start to take her hands. But then Aunt Amy came in and it was no use. It was all hurried and unended like that, those last few days. But I wanted to get them through as soon as possible. I kept thinking how it would be when I came back.

They all saw me off at the station, even Aleck. It was quite a family party. I couldn't kiss her because that wasn't fair. But everyone waved, and when the train moved at last and she was still standing there, I felt ashamed of any doubts I had ever had. She looked so tall, standing there beside Aunt Amy. "*Si tu as de la veine!*" said the cheese-eating soldier beside me. "*C'est agaçant!*" and he took a long gulp of wine.

And so, for another two months, I wrote letters.

[*95*]

James Shore must have been amused by his, if he read them, for I took my part of investigator very seriously—seriously enough to very nearly get me a beating in one plant as an employer's spy. And my hands hardened, and, with them, a part of my mind—for De Vecchi's workshop had been like a brawling family, but, where I went, we dealt in metal, not wood, and the life itself had a different grain. I thought I could tell Carlo unsuspected things about his engines when I saw him again— I began to think, ingenuously, there were even things I might be able to tell James Shore. I had nothing from them, but then I didn't expect it— weren't we all going to meet in Paris in the fall? I even stayed an extra two days in Essen because I ran into a little Englishman who said he was an inventor and I suddenly saw myself, returning, with an Edison in my pocket for James Shore's private use. But he was so unnecessarily wary that I gave him up in the end. And, on the way back to Paris, I slept and slept and slept, for I was tired.

I arrived late in the evening and went to the hotel at once. But they were not there, and the only forwarding address was James Shore's bank in London. So I cursed the stupidity of hotels and the casualness of the rich very loudly to myself, but, as I cursed, I feared. Then I went back to my rooms and found six postcards from Violet and the letter saying she was engaged to Charles Morton and they were sailing home. I could have forgiven the letter, for it was like letters in books and full of the heavy phrases that the young love so well to use. I could not forgive the postcards, for they were beyond my comprehension. Even Carlotta would not have sent me a postcard of the Tower if she had gone to London with her courier.

I thought of the last two months, and I laughed, as I hoped, very bitterly. It had been such an easy trap. James Shore had used me as a buffer against the Europe he instinctively distrusted, while I had been useful as a buffer. When I became an annoyance, he had neatly and expeditiously removed me, almost at my own request. There might even be a check awaiting me at his Paris correspondents', if I turned in my report, for James Shore had an honesty of his own. But I would not go and fetch it. Violet could have her Charles Morton and I would go to the devil. Only not to Dicky's devil, for that would remind me too much.

So I did, and it was harder work than I expected, but it served. I wrote wild letters to Violet and tore them up unread—I was not even sure she would get them—they would be so easy to stop. When I had time for thought, I rubbed salt in the wound. I could see the elder Morton, with his face of a distinguished horse, sitting at James Shore's table, while James Shore gave him a cigar. The Mortons liked to think themselves dynastic people —but the man from the West had won, as he always won. It had been a new game to him, doubtless, and he had watched and listened for a long time without taking part in it. But, when he had taken part in it, he had had the chips.

All over Paris, they were starting to take the Exposition down. When I was not being Rudolf Rassendyl, I tried very hard to think of the Shores as another exhibit—something as unreal and passing as the Street of the Nations, as the Arabs and Danes who came and went away. One must not touch the exhibits—that had been my mistake. But even as I thought the words, I knew that they were false.

I met Dicky, by chance, in a café, and we quarreled, bitterly and definitely, for he called Violet

[*98*]

an "*allumeuse*." He had made his formal demand
and it had been refused without ceremony—and
he was perfectly right, according to his lights, which
only made me the angrier. But, with that quarrel,
I knew that a door was shut. You have to work
very hard to keep your place in that world, if you
are not born to it—and I had had my chance. At
one moment, I might even have formed a more or
less permanent attachment with one of two ladies
who had come to an age to be interested in young
men's careers. It was chic, in that year, to harbor
a minor poet or a member of the Institute, and,
while a stray American was a little daring, stranger
things had occurred.

Once those things are begun, they grow into re-
spectability with the years. I can see myself now,
at fifty, grown a little heavy at the stern and almost French, the man who has the particular
chair in the salon between half-past four and
seven—the old permitted caller with the ribbon
in his buttonhole, whose eyes drift a little hungrily
to the red, peasant face of the maid who brings
in the cakes. Or that other man, a little battered,
at the races, not quite a tout, not entirely a professional gossip, dazzling the young Charles Whip-

ley Mortons, for a moment, with his stories of the days when Paris was Paris and letting them pay for his dinner at Larue's. I can see them clearly, for I might have been either. But Violet came to Paris instead.

Even so, when I came back, one morning, and the concierge gave me the smudged, blue telegram, my heart leaped foolishly, thinking it must be from her. But it was from Mother instead, and I caught the Rome Express. Carlo had had the first of his hemorrhages, and that was the time they were sure he could not live.

PART III

WHEN I met James Shore's daughter again, it
was after many things had happened. I am not
telling the story of a rise in the world or the break-
down of a civilization or how Mother and Time got
their genius after all. I am telling her story and
mine, or as much of it as I can. As much as I can,
because no confession of life has ever been the
truth. We try very hard to tell the truth, but, even
as we do so, it alters. The words are no sooner
spoken than they are false, not from any wish to
deceive but because life has moved on, like the

[*103*]

waters of a river, while we were speaking. The waters replace the waters forever, but that is not the same.

Fate hangs on very small things, and I nearly decided to send young Guimard to Vienna to buy the Obenheim collection. He needed the experience, and it sounded like one of those typical magpie nests that certain collectors accumulate. But I wanted the Ingres drawings, if they existed. And, at the last moment, I decided to go myself and run up and see Carlo at Anderesplatz afterward. His letters were good and he was gaining weight, but, for five years, we had thought him cured.

I was late in getting to the train, for the London mail had just come in, and with it a letter from Richards. There was trouble about the Cuyp again, and they wanted another expert. Experts always frightened Richards—he had not yet learned the lesson that, wherever there is an expert, there is another expert to contradict him. Nevertheless Richards was invaluable, for he really knew and liked modern painting. They hadn't been able to get along with him, at Dyner's; he had been too rude. But his rudeness was an asset, if properly handled. He had been appallingly rude to me, the first time I had ever seen him, with his yellow hair, his made tie, his long nose, white as a spermaceti candle, and the cardboard over the holes in the soles of his boots. All the same, he had made our London gallery. I wondered, as I often did, if he hated me for taking him away from the made tie, the reader's ticket to the British Museum, the Socialist Club in Hammersmith, and the freedom of his poverty to look only at the pictures he liked and mumble "Swill!" at the rest. The "Swill!" was partly a pose, of course, but a valuable one. It made the department-store proprietor buy the two Manets—he was not accustomed to being told that his Winterhalters were swill.

Young Guimard pursued me as far as the door with questions, but I finally managed to get rid of him without hurting his feelings. It would do him good to handle things for a while, and he could call in his uncle, if necessary. The old man had never quite got over our moving from the Rue de Seine, and the London branch of the business he regarded with acute suspicion. But he was perfectly sound in his own line and he looked impressive. He had his house at Meudon—an inordinately ugly little villa, with the rosebushes and the graveled garden of his retirement—but once a week he would come in and potter about the quarter he had left. He would go to the great sales, too, though he did not bid any more.

I felt perfectly sure that he did not believe in our success, but it had happened and he accepted it. He would not die rich, for I had bought him out at the right time, but he would leave a very solid sum to Jules and Jules' sisters. And money was a lasting thing, in spite of Richards and his painters. It had its own satisfactions, and they were both solid and reckless, once you accepted the game.

All the same, I felt tired, in the taxi. It had been a busy winter, both in Paris and London. We had established Van Meeren, and the Chinese show had been a miraculous success. I gave Van Meeren five years, with luck, but there wasn't any doubt about his vogue, and the five years would make us money. And the Chinese show had been real. I had known that as soon as I saw it, though it had been Richards's idea. They called us theatrical and undignified—they called me a Yankee showman—but we were able to do things they could not do. Next year we would give up the small stuff entirely—it was profitable but a nuisance. Or perhaps we could find an outlet for it—another shop in the Rue de Seine, under another name. There was also New York to be considered—the trend was there, undoubtedly, but I wasn't quite sure about it yet. I would have to do it myself—there was never any other way but doing things yourself. Old Guimard would have been content to stay in the Rue de Seine.

Yes, we'd done very well indeed, but we must do still better. "It doesn't matter whether people are nice to you—it matters whether you're somebody or not," a girl named Violet Shore had said, years ago. Well, Enid would never forgive me for not devoting the London gallery exclusively to Arthur Lakeside's water-colors, but there was nothing there. At least I'd managed to save Carlo from the room in Rome—the room that Mother, in her terror, had automatically arranged to remind one ever so slightly of the dying Keats. Young death is always romantic and young illness touching, but when I had seen the dark hairs growing on my brother's arm, I had known that he was a man—and a man should live before he dies.

I had managed that, at least, where Mother, for all her love, would have kept him the young Keats of the legend to the end. It was different from love and much simpler. Perhaps I would get married, one of these days—successful men did. I had thought of it a couple of times, once for ease and once for desire, but there hadn't been time— there was always Carlo to plan for, and we were rising in the world. Oh, I'd gone through the gestures of love, when they were necessary, and once they had almost been genuine, with Gerda. And for some years I had kept a queer set of clippings in my desk—clippings from American papers and of no importance to anyone, except that they mentioned the name of Mrs. Charles Whipley Morton. There was one photograph at a horse show—the little boy had strong legs and his father's face. The girl's picture I'd never seen. I had torn them all up and burned them—when was it?—I couldn't remember. But it must have been just before we moved to the Rue de La Boétie. Gerda hadn't been jealous of Carlo, but she had been jealous of something. And that was nonsense, because I had burned the clippings. I hadn't even thought of them for a long time.

I was still thinking of Gerda as I hurried through the waiting room of the station to catch my express. But, in spite of the hurry, something jerked my head to the left. And there was a small tribe of porters, hurrying also, and behind them were James Shore's daughter and James Shore.

There were three other people with them, a maid, a woman who might be anything, and a man who must be a secretary, but I did not look at those. My eyes and Violet's met, and we knew each other. She was smaller than I remembered her, and her clothes were not the clothes of the picture I had burned. I thought, with a horrible pang of relief, "She's older, it's gone." Then she threw back her head impatiently at something the secretary said, and it was like the flash of a mirror in my eyes. I can find no other simile for that blind, bright shock. The face may change, and the body, but certain gestures remain. "*Mais, depêchez vous!*" I said angrily, to my porter, though there was plenty of time.

He grumbled, and I prodded him, and he fairly threw my bags on board the train. So I undertipped him, and he told me what he thought. I knew I was being ridiculous, but that did not help.

It was perfectly reasonable that we should see each other again in the comfortless anonymity of a railway station, with the clang and the steam and the swarming, the white-faced clocks and the sad baying of tourists. It was even appropriate. But it was not what I had planned.

After the train had started, I gazed at myself in the little glass of my compartment. I was Gareth Grant, well-known, international dealer in works of art. Not so well known yet as I meant to be—but, in twelve years, I'd made a name and sums of money, and kept my brother alive. I had on dark, respectable clothes, my hair was neatly parted, my stick in the rack. I looked, on the whole, like a prosperous seal. I wasn't pompous yet, but that would come. It made me angry to think of it. It made me angrier still to think of the Shores. For I had no doubt at all that they were on the train, and little that they were going through to Vienna. It seemed an unwarrantable intrusion of Fate. I had thought of our meeting times enough, for I was my mother's son. But it wasn't to happen like this. I was busy—I was changed—I had made myself a new shell to live in. No, I wasn't glad to see James Shore's daughter again.

I settled myself in the compartment and picked up the paper I hadn't had time to read. Mme. la Ctesse. de Saugres had given a reception in her mansion on the Avenue du Bois de Boulogne, in honor of her sister, Miss Mabel Shong of Milwaukee. I had not attended that wedding, though the countess had come to the gallery once. She was plump with china-blue eyes and a very firm chin. Tante 'Line would not defeat her and neither would Dicky, in spite of the house on the Avenue du Bois—I could see those plump heels drubbing on the floor in a tantrum of a sort that Dicky could not face. Indeed, I felt rather sorry for Dicky, after I'd seen her. With all his faults, he was human, and she had the strong resilient stupidity of one of those floating jellies that eat, excrete, and divide, in an endless cycle of life, without thought or delusion. It was perfectly fair, of course, but Dicky had once been my friend and I didn't intend to sell her any pictures if I could help it. I was finished with that world, except as vendor or buyer. James Shore's daughter had done that much for me, at least.

She had done more than she had imagined. I thought of the years since I had seen her. I had

[*111*]

sometimes forgot why I was climbing. Then I would think of James Shore, lugging his tripod and his camera case, from town to dusty town, and remember. I wondered what had driven him as Carlo and something besides Carlo had driven me. Perhaps I could get close to it, if we met again now. But I wasn't sure that I wanted to. I had met a good many of them now, in my trade—the bold Jews and the timid ones, the Scotsman with the actor's streak in him and the man with the nose like a parrot and the thick eyebrows who bought and bought and bought the works of the dead. James Shore had helped me to deal with them, though he didn't know it. But the past was the past, and I'd changed more than the parting in my hair. I'd go into the *wagon restaurant*, get an early dinner, and work the rest of the evening on the papers in my bag. The Shores certainly wouldn't go to the first service, and I could avoid them in Vienna easily enough.

But when I went down the swaying aisle, between the small tables, they were already seated. However, I was across the aisle and farther down. I had only to look at the secretary and the woman who might be anything, for the other backs were

[*112*]

turned toward me. And even that was difficult, for opposite me sat the other occupant of my compartment—a painstaking young German who, obviously, was only too eager to improve his English at my expense. But when Violet leaned forward to speak to her father, I could see a corner of her face.

"Second ser-ving is better as first ser-ving," said my German, articulating very slowly and carefully. "But you like first ser-ving, yes?"

"Yes," I said, looking at the menu and knowing there would be veal.

"So," he said, with apparent satisfaction. "You like first ser-ving better. That is inter-esting. Always you have liked first ser-ving better?"

"Yes," I said, wishing I had brought my newspaper with me and that Violet would take off her hat. I wanted to see her hair again. My German leaned forward.

"We Germans, we dravel much," he confided. "I dravel much. We think second ser-ving much better. But you are not a German. You are Swiss— English—American?"

"Not exactly," I said desperately, "I mean— well, I'm more or less of a mongrel, I suppose."

[*113*]

His painstaking face looked shocked.

"But no," he said, even more slowly, "I have an-thro-pology studied. You cannot be a Mongol. You have not the eyes, like so," and, without the slightest warning, he seriously pushed up the corners of his own eyes with his thumbs to make them look slant.

It was too sudden. I laughed, wildly and youthfully and as I had not laughed in years. I could not help it, even when I saw his face change from solemnity to bewilderment and then to affront.

"You are not po-lite," he said, finally. "*Ganz gut*—I vaste not my con-ver-sation," and he devoted himself sulkily to his food.

I apologized, but it was half in a dream. The laugh had broken a tension, and I had been even more pompous than I thought. One got that way, with success. It wasn't serious or fatal that James Shore's daughter and I should meet again—the glance, in the station, had taken me back twelve years, but that was over. I'd imagined our meeting many times, in those years. But now it had happened—and there was nothing to be done but laugh at a harmless bore and eat veal in a swaying train.

For two pins and a small matter of pride, I would go over this minute, shake hands with the Shores, and ask Violet about her children. I remembered the hot months of that Roman spring when Carlo had been so ill and when, painfully, inescapably, and whenever I was alone, I had pictured to myself, step by step, the Mortons' English wedding tour—the flowers in the cabin of the steamship, the flowers in the hotels. That was gone, with youth's self-torture. We could both be civilized, now. I ought to know, by this time, what happened to people who took life too seriously. They were not broken by it, as in Mother's novels. They were merely made redundantly absurd.

So, when they got up to go and she turned and nodded, guardedly, I returned the nod and inclined my head toward James Shore. I could almost see his lips move in the "Well, Colonel—" though he did not speak, or else I did not catch it in the roar of the train. He looked taller and drier than ever, but there was a slowness in his step, and the skin of his face was sallow. The little procession passed down the aisle and was gone.

"I vill only ask you one question," said my

German, after a while. "You are not a Mongol, but you seem not quite Anglo-Saxon. Are you, berhaps, Indian-blooded?"

I rose and bowed, in spite of the train.

"*Monsieur*," I said, "*je suis le plus grand imbécile du monde. C'est héréditaire*," and I left him with his mouth open, looking at his bill.

So I wasn't surprised, as I passed on down the train, to nod again to a face and stop in a compartment door. They had about half a car to themselves, though there were only five of them. It seemed natural to be smoking one of James Shore's cigars again. It seemed natural to chat with Violet about postimpressionism and Votes for Women, about the new college-professor President and auction bridge. There were names we mentioned, and she drew me out on my subject—I even became heated about the postimpressionists, and she listened and smiled with that smile of intelligent interest which I had seen assumed upon other faces, on similar occasions, in my trade. It was all very natural, and something kept laughing and laughing in my head. I had imagined great cataclysms and superb convulsions of nature, and they simply did not exist. There was no scene to be made, only conversation—and, as we made it, we jolted, faintly and in unison, with the motion of the wheels, and, outside, the black night streamed past.

Now and then I would catch a glimpse of my own face in the glass of the window, pink and animated, like a face in a magic lantern. It seemed pleased to be talking to old acquaintances, but neither triumphant nor disturbed. Presently it might yawn, for the train was hot. Mrs. Charles Whipley Morton had yawned a moment before but suppressed it, tactfully. She seemed exceedingly tactful for so handsome a woman. In the last dozen years a number of things had happened to her, including marriage and birth, but one did not speak of these things, on a train, even to an old acquaintance. Only James Shore said what he liked and kept silent when he wished. But then he had that privilege, for he was not well.

There was something badly the matter with that dry, masterful countenance, now I saw it closer. The flesh of the big nose had fallen away, as it may sometimes with the old, but the rest of the face was puffy and not with health. It was like seeing a sick eagle or a sick desert. There was no room for the easy small-change of emotion we pass from one hand to the other for the poor dear boy with the cough or the brave little woman who has so much to bear. There was only room for strangeness and a sort of superstitious bewilderment. If the lizard, with his mail and his cold blood, shall also suffer the pang, what is there left for a man?

And yet it did not seem to concern him, though he took the drops from the bottle openly enough.

"There was a man with a medicine show once, selling Kickapoo Spring Tonic," he said, when he had swallowed. "Tastes a little the same. He claimed it was herbs, in general, dug off Injun graves. But I guess it was the Jamaica ginger that did the work."

"Now, Father!" said his daughter, dutifully, in her cultured American voice.

"Oh, I'm going," he said, a little restlessly, "I'm going to see the man—what's his name?—always makes me think of the Dutchman's. But that was before your time."

"Dr. Rotenfahn, Father. You know who he is, of course, Garry."

"Of course," I said. James Shore turned his eye on me—the eye of the American of his time, apologetic for being sick when that is a woman's business.

"Always thought we had plenty of doctors on our side," he said. "But it seems as if they liked to pass you around."

"Well, you'll be in safe hands with him," I said, briskly. "He's supposed to be the best kidney man in the world."

"Kidney man," said James Shore, musingly. "Sounds funny, doesn't it?" He chuckled. "Oh, I'm in safe hands," he said, with his dry smile. "Violet sees to that."

"He's a much better patient than he sounds," said Violet, brightly.

It was all like that—quite natural and unreal. I asked for Aleck and Aunt Amy—I even asked for Charles Morton. They were well, they were well, they were well. No, I hadn't heard of Aleck's second marriage—for that matter, I hadn't heard of his first—but I expressed suitable pleasure. "Well, he gets married quite a bit," said James Shore, without any apparent humor, and Violet laughed, tolerantly. I saw the pictures of the children. Then the nurse came in for James Shore, though it was not late.

I stood, for a moment, with Violet in the corridor.

"He doesn't look so terribly badly, does he?" she said, in the way that question is always asked.

"Not a bit," I said. "Of course I don't know whom you've seen. But Rotenfahn has a magnificent reputation."

"I'm glad you think so," she said, in a preoccupied voice. "It was hard, getting him away. Well, we'll see you in Vienna, won't we? We'll be at the Splendide."

"Oh, of course," I said. "And, naturally, if there's anything I can do . . ."

She thanked me, and we stood looking. Then she said, "Father's glad to see you. And we'd love to meet Mrs. Grant."

"There isn't any, at present," I said. "But I've met Mr. Morton. It's quite a bond."

I saw a flash of exasperation in her eyes. It was the first real thing I had seen in either of us. Then it was smoothed out, wiped away by the new expression—the one I had been studying all the while in the compartment—the competent, smiling countenance that all great ladies everywhere turn to the sun.

[*120*]

"You haven't changed much, Garry," she said, lightly. "But we read about things, you know—even in New York. I'm glad you've done so well."

"Oh, I've done very well," I said. "It's a fascinating story. They haven't called me the Napoleon of the art world yet, but I daresay they may, in time. With proper inducements."

"You always did twist things, didn't you?" she said. "I remember that. Well, good-night."

"Good-night," I said and went back to my compartment and my German. He was snoring firmly, and as I undressed I wondered if he had a theory as to the various relationships between men and women. I decided that he probably did and that it was wrong.

All the same, I had been challenged and I accepted the challenge. If we were to meet as acquaintances, we should meet. It would be an interesting experiment, and prove that Gerda was wrong. Besides, the Obenheim business was going to take me longer than I expected. The two Obenheim sisters were both canny and sentimental— they talked of dear Uncle Adolf's beautiful collection with tears in their voices and had to be sustained by chocolate and cakes whenever I asked a single, definite question. Then they would show me three appalling clocks, a photograph of Uncle Adolf at the age of nine, and an Ingres drawing—and sink, exhausted, into their chairs. Oh, yes, there were other drawings—Uncle Adolf had drawn, himself. There were paintings, too, in the country house—but that was a long trip—one had to go in the train. They had not been there since Uncle Adolf died—it had been too painful—but the caretaker was very good and wrote them every week about the garden. I thought of possible Grecos moldering away in a flooded cellar—Uncle Adolf had spent eight years in Spain and brought back lots of queer pictures and a beautiful shawl for each sister—and yearned to break into the house with a set of burglar's tools. But it couldn't be done, and I knew it—the only thing was patience. Krutschler had already tried to bully them, and obviously it hadn't worked. So I settled down for a long siege, told myself that Uncle Adolf, from his photograph, was just the sort of man who would have collected Greco, and, after a suitable interval, called at the Splendide.

There were people at tea already, in the high rooms overlooking the green garden, the afternoon

that I called, and I sat in a corner and nibbled a
dry cake and talked to a lean Englishwoman.
She was dry and unsustaining as the cake, but I
didn't mind, for I was watching Violet. Yes, she
had come a long way. She handled her animals very
well, I thought—the Mortons must be pleased with
her manner. It spoke of the adventures of the rich
but cultivated—the adventure of waking in strange
cities, but always in the same hotel, and sometimes taking a foreign street car, for a lark—the
adventure of talking to writers and musicians and
explorers quite simply and even humbly and
putting them at their ease whether they wished
to be there or not—the adventure of being friendly
with nice little people one met and forgot and
democratic, within limits, to one's butcher and
one's chauffeur. One does not assert one's prerog-
atives, one takes them as a matter of course. It
was a quiet little dinner for the ambassador—just
a few old friends—and, afterwards, Kreisler played.

It made me ache a little, for her beauty was now
mature and, in every line and aspect, it demanded
a rawer splendor, a more barbaric triumph. She
would not have been ridiculous on a throne of
painted steel, with the fruits of plenty at her feet

and a golden wheat-ear in her hand. But she poured tea very well. I wondered if anywhere now she still had the nugget from the mine.

"Jolly good complexion for an American," said the Englishwoman beside me, with that intimate rudeness which is the birthright of certain of the English. "Pukka, too. Knew her in London. But it'll go, of course. All American women's do. Too many complexion creams and that ghastly central heating." She touched her own leather cheek. "Rode to hounds all my life and never used anything but soap and water," she said. "Best thing in the world for it. Tell my girls so. But they're lazy. Rather pay two guineas a jar for imported slops."

She cackled like a marsh hen and rose. "Well, m'dear," she said to Violet, "decent of you to have us. Thanks awf'ly. Must come down to Chumbles for a week-end, when you're in London. Always there for the shooting, y'know. Now where's Brinsley—oh, there you are. Just telling Mrs. Morton . . ."

The large, pink, white-haired gentleman bowed over Violet's hand as he does in the Beerbohm cartoon, only there the hand is a royal one. He

[*124*]

said a few words to Violet in the voice I had heard described, unflatteringly yet admiringly, by Dicky and his friends, when I knew them. Then the party broke up.

"Oh, Garry, you're not going?" said Violet. "Why, I've hardly spoken to you. I didn't know there'd be such a crowd. There won't be again. It tires Father. But they were just passing through, and I had to do something. Won't you come back and dine with us? Just a black tie, you know, and very informal."

I should have declined, but again I felt a challenge. So I accepted, instead, and after dinner we talked. It was like Paris over again, only it was not. The big cigar box lay on the marble-topped table in the same sort of suite in the same sort of hotel. There was nothing gone but Aunt Amy, and the first youth from both of us, and the health of his body from James Shore. But the cables had come from America already, and Mr. Barker, the secretary, had brought his typewriter with him. I felt half as if I were dreaming, half as if I were very old.

The hotel was a quiet one, and the main sitting room of the suite had a small balcony, looking

down on the garden. We sat there, after dinner.
For a while James Shore sat with us; then he
went to his secretary. The trip had tired him a good
deal, and his letters were in arrears. There was
brandy in the glass I had, but I didn't drink it.
It wasn't necessary to drink it. From somewhere
distant, faint, gay, and incredibly thin, across the
murmur of the city, came tiny music, music
made for very small, very brilliant dolls with pink
cheeks and silver dolmans, sloping shoulders and
curled wooden hair.

We listened to it and talked, and, slowly, the
unreality between us faded. I told her about the
new Countess de Saugres, and she smiled. "Poor
Dicky," she said. "I must have been a horrible
girl in those days." She stopped for a minute.
"It wasn't all Father's fault," she said, in a low
voice. "Of course there's no use explaining."

"No," I said.

"That's nice of you, Garry," she said, with an
odd content in her voice, and, as she lay back in
her chair, I looked at her through the dim light
and thought that there could be no more terrible
phrase than the old one, "two people made for
each other." For, with evening and the music of

the dolls, the old ache revived and I knew the truth. We were made for each other, but not for each other and the lives we lived, each other and the other desires we had. She would not ask for a glass of cold milk again, for the old impatience with Europe was gone. Indeed she said as much, in that frank, new voice.

"It seems all wrong," she said, "with the children away and being worried about Father. But it's pleasant to be over again. I haven't for years, except England."

She smiled.

"Were you in Rome three years ago, Garry?" she said. "Around the first week in October? I thought I saw you. Just as we were going to the station."

"No," I said. "Not that October."

"That's queer," she said. "I was sure of it. It was just a glimpse, and we were going. You had on a brown suit and you were smoking. It looked very like you."

"No," I said, deliberately, "I wasn't there."

"Well," she said, with what was almost laughter, "you ought to know. But it's funny, isn't it? Oh, quite a long while, I thought I'd see you, in America. As I was turning a corner or going along a street. Sometimes it was important, too."

Her voice came from the dimness without color, like water moving slowly, without purpose and yet to an instinctive end.

"Oh, well," she said, "I'm talking nonsense. I suppose I do, a good deal. You might ask Charles' sister," and she laughed, in the new way.

But I had seen Charles Morton's last picture, and I did not have to ask certain questions. The face had grown more solid, but it was little changed. It still stared at life with the emphasis of a halfback —life was a game that gentlemen always won because they made the rules. The years had given the eyes neither shrewdness nor subtlety, and the mouth was fuller than before. It did not surprise me particularly that such a face should rule—I had knocked around too much, by now, for that. But I thought, with a mean satisfaction, how the first Charles Morton—that sharp little trader from England—would have fleeced the owner of that face.

"I'm afraid I don't know her," I said. "But I wouldn't, unless she collects."

"No," said Violet. "She's charities and politics.

[*128*]

She married in Newport—one of the Ganelons. She thinks I'm rather bad for Charles. It made things rather trying, that first summer." She drew a long breath. "Oh, I've learned a great many things, Garry," she said. "A great many things. But she won't do that again."

The doll's music rose and fell, and we neither of us said anything for a moment. Violet's dress rustled as she moved.

"It's queer, liking being over here so much," she said. "It's as if I'd been asleep a long time. I don't know why it is."

So we sat in another silence, until I rose to go. But, all night, the faint, tiny music hummed in my head. It was very faint, but when I woke I still heard it. They called it the "Frühlingswalzer"— but I knew they called it wrongly. It was not the music of spring. I wondered if James Shore had heard it, as he lay in his bed alone. He had come a long way to hear it, but not so far as I.

And meanwhile the sun rose and set and the Obenheim sisters annoyed me and I carried on complicated negotiations with Richards and Guimard by telegraph for the Chalfont tapestries, and Violet got letters from her children and I made the acquaintance of Mr. Allan Barker. He was a nice young man with severe steel spectacles and a pleasant smile, and when he spoke of James Shore he called him "the Chief."

It was a new breed to me, and I was interested. He wore a fraternity pin inconspicuously on the vest of his dark blue suit, and he had a profound belief in diplomas, courses, and advertising. By these means all things might be acquired, from colloquial Czech to a knowledge of the human soul. I must say that both his French and his German, though sterile, were entirely efficient. He carefully went to beer gardens to improve his languages, and to art galleries to broaden his personality, and, when he had nothing else to do, he studied something called the Benjamin Franklin Plan.

It was, as he explained to me, a mental training school for potential leaders, and he showed me the drab, expensive books with pride. There were problems in Merchandising and problems in Management—there may have been problems in Mousetraps and Muchness for all I know. He had thumbed and rethumbed the first volumes and done all the problems at the ends of the chapters until he got them right. "It's all so darn *practical!*"

he assured me, earnestly, as he showed me how to run a paper business at a paper profit. "You see, in the first place, it's a Plan. Everything's planned. They give you regular exams., too, just like college ones, and if there's any individual difficulty, they write you a personal letter. Then, of course, when you're through, you get a dignified certificate—but it's the experience that counts." It struck me as being a practically foolproof way of making money, for it would always be easy enough to get someone to write the books.

Nevertheless Mr. Barker fascinated me, for he was the first person I had met who believed in business because of the printed word. The acts of making, buying, and selling were not merely interesting or profitable—they were virtuous in themselves. They must be so because of college and other men's fathers and the advertisements and the Benjamin Franklin Plan. He didn't quite talk about knights in shining armor, but he had a whole new terminology for the most ordinary commercial acts—a terminology of heroism and struggle and sacrifice. It made me feel rather awed, for it seemed to me to bear no relation whatever to life, and yet it was obviously a religion. Above the high altar hung two huge pasteboard masks, Personality and Opportunity, and to these Allan Barker prayed. I had seen people sweat and toil and do evil for money or power, but never before for pasteboard, and I was at a loss.

I asked James Shore about him, and he grunted and said, "Oh, Barker? Well, Colonel, when my grandmother got older, I hear she took to a fox terrier. He was a good deal of a fool but kind of company, and he'd carry her newspaper back from the post office in his mouth. That was back in New England, of course. Well, I'm not so young as I was."

"He says it's a wonderful opportunity, being so close to the Chief," I said, though I could not reproduce the automatic boyishness of that voice.

"Well," said James Shore, tolerantly, "he thinks you've got quite a personality, Colonel. Artistic but businesslike. He talked to me about it the other night."

He smoked for a while in silence.

"I wonder if I better leave him some money?" he said. "I suppose they'd get it away from him, but you hate to think of a fellow like that when he finds out it's none of it so."

After that, I felt a trifle sorry for Mr. Barker. But it was hard to feel sorry for anyone at once so respectful and so assured. He treated me with a hearty, companionable deference that made me feel like a centenarian. With Violet, his manner held a hint of chivalric protection, for, as James Shore's daughter and Charles Morton's wife, she was triply sacrosanct, as a woman, a mother, and a symbol. Now and then I would catch him looking at her beauty with a certain appraisal in his eye. It was beyond criticism, for it belonged to Big Chiefs, but it tended toward the extreme. You could feel him deciding, privately, on a somewhat less conspicuous model—something with the quiet lines and subdued finish of an imitation maplewood chair. I don't know why that used to irritate me so much.

His eye was more speculative when it fell upon Miss Sunding, the nurse. She had brown, vivid eyes and an excellent skin, and she was one of the few completely competent people I have ever known. I imagine, if they both hadn't been working for the Big Chief, that he would have liked to try and hold her hand and tell her about his ambitions. As it was, his manner with her was a little breathless though entirely correct. There could have been few better people to confide in than Elsa Sunding —she had not learned her business on the Benjamin Franklin Plan, and she had the capacity for silence of a well. She was, perhaps, thirty years old, and I knew, instinctively, after a week's acquaintance, that she had both a story and a secret. And, whatever the story was, it would be worth knowing, for it dealt with life, not words.

Violet rather disliked her on the whole, as women will. They were both strong, though after different fashions. I could have taken Violet's word for it once, but I couldn't now—and that gives one measure of our change. I would have enjoyed taking Violet's word and disliking Elsa Sunding—but that was gone, with the posters that had been on the kiosks that spring in Paris and my lust to be a Richard Harding Davis hero. It did not help us at all that such things were gone, for nothing helps love. It did not help us at all that we were changed. It merely wove the net tighter.

There was the gay city and the music and the kindliness—I didn't know it well, it was foreign to me as well. I remember standing on a street corner, one morning, and watching a cavalry regiment pass, with its kettledrums. They were to be dead in two years, they and their horses, but we did not know it, in the crowd, and if we had known it, we would not have believed. Even when the guns went by, I did not think of them firing—they were so long and clean. We will not think of them again, that way, in our time—but I wondered, idly, why none of the new painters had yet thought of guns for design, and turned away, for Violet was to meet me, and it marked a step in our journey.

There was a little church on a side street, where no tourists came. It had a small fenced graveyard, with paths, and a bench and trees. It was near the hotel, and yet it might have been in another world. The graves were old graves, for the most part, and it was all very quiet, not sad at all, merely green and still, as if the dust rested well. I was there before her and wandered about for a few minutes, reading the names of the sleepers. There was one inscription in Latin to four brothers, Italians and musicians, who had come from Turin, two centuries before, to sing and play for the pleasure of another emperor than Franz Josef. Three had died the same year, apparently in some plague, the fourth had survived them forty years, but had returned to lie beside them at last. "Remembering the days of his youth and his sweet-throated companions" the inscription said, "he chose rather to rest with them, in another country, than with wife and child, at home." I thought of them with friendliness, for they also were adventurers and strangers. It was a queer place for an idyll, but I was not planning an idyll. James Shore's daughter and I had gone beyond that.

I turned from the inscription, and she was coming through the little gate, very splendid, in soft grey, with the high peaked shoulders of the time.

"You're very beautiful today," I said, idly and lightly, while the doll's music hummed in my head.

She gave me a quick glance. "I'm coming awake," she said. "I told you I felt like that, didn't I? Well, it's true." She stopped for a moment and smoothed an edge of moss on a stone with her glove and looked at the stain. "I keep doing things like that," she said. "Queer. Now don't tell me I've spoiled my gloves."

"I shan't," I said, and we walked up and down the paths and talked of James Shore's illness—was not that why we had met? Then suddenly she said,

"This is a nice place, Garry. I'm glad you found it. Do you have to have a place to get away from people, too? It's a funny question, I suppose."

I thought of Anderesplatz. When we'd got there, Carlo and I, eleven years before, I was nearly desperate, for Carlo came flat on his back, like an image carved above a tomb. It was evening, and I could still remember the pools of sunset on the snow and how I could only think of blood on a handkerchief and that cough that sounds as if it tore green wood, not flesh, and the wood suffered. But afterwards, and for many years, it had been such a place for me. You could think in easy phrases as you went up to it—the Great White Plague and the Laughter of the Doomed—but when you got there, you stopped. There was always something monkish about it, in spite of the feverish love affairs that flicker through all sanatoria. Have you ever melted lead and poured the drops into deep snow? They take strange shapes and sink, and the next snowfall covers them—the crust on the snow seems more solid than the lead. There was a solidity to that long line of peaked wooden roofs—a bare solidity, like the planking of a ship. Love was brittle and molten beside it, and one did not think of nobility or the irony of man, but of something else.

It was not Mother's climate, and it irked her that it should not be. But she had written a book called *Edelweiss* to make up for it—it was largely concerned with a mother who loses her son to the Great White Plague and adopts a Swiss village instead. The villagers called the heroine "Mutter Edelweiss," and many quite healthy people still wrote in to say that it had helped them. When Carlo read it, it sent his temperature up for two days, for Mother had used scraps from his letters. But he wrote her very charmingly about it, and it was always in his room when she came. I wondered if he had it still. He was back there now, but he had had life, in between. I had not had so much of life, in those years, though I had done business.

I told Violet something of this, and she nodded. "Yes," she said. "When I was having the children, those two summers, I used to make Billings drive me out—oh, you wouldn't know the place—it's on the wrong side of the island and nobody's built there, but from the top of the road you can see the water a long way. It isn't breakers—just water. From one place you can't see anything but marshes

and the water coming in, with white at the edge
where it breaks. Charles never liked me to do it.
They'd have said I was meeting a lover, but they
couldn't when they knew I was having a child.
Billings used to get awfully tired of waiting, but he
was afraid to make the horses kick. I told Charles
the sea air was good for me, but it wasn't that. I
even went there in the rain, once or twice, though
it made Billings angry, not to speak of the Mortons.
They weren't so concerned, the second time—after
all, I'd had Charles Junior, then. But things like
that upset them." She paused. "What nonsense
I'm talking, Garry. But it's fun to talk nonsense
again."

I was still under the spell of seeing her sitting
in the carriage, with her gloved hands tightening
on the robe and her eyes looking out over the
water, while the coachman's back looked uneasy
and the very sleek horses jingled their harness as
they stood.

"Good God!" I said. "Hasn't any of it been
realler than that?" I hardly knew my voice. She
put her hand on my arm for a moment and with-
drew it.

"Well," she said, with a touch of laughter, "it's

been exciting. I'm not a clever person, Garry—it's hard for me to explain. But I wasn't proud when I went there—I didn't mean to be proud. They'd had their things a long time, and I knew it. It wasn't like Aubenel and Dicky's family—that was lovely, but it was like pictures out of a book. And Charles' father was a darling. He gave me the emeralds himself." She stopped. "Only they're *fussy* people," she said in a low voice, for it was obviously a heresy. "I don't know how to explain it. They've got time and they've been to places and they're used to the servants and the houses. But if you put them in Gunflint—well, most of them wouldn't get out."

"Not Charles?" I said.

"Oh, Charles," she said, with a laugh. "Charles would get out. Charles would get as far as Denver. I don't mean to be horrid about Charles. But we had a little dispute before I sailed, and I'm just a trifle annoyed with Charles, to tell you the truth. He will waste time—oh—on people of no importance. Well, I'm not a child." But something in her face looked hurt, and I cursed Charles Morton for hurting it. I could guess very well who the people of no importance were. But I murmured

[*140*]

something instead about the greatness of the
Morton name, and she looked pleased.

"Yes," she said. "That's fun. And it can be
more than that. Charles is a little too close to it
to realize. And I see some things better than he
does. Of course there have to be changes—and the
President's a radical—but politics don't mean very
much, anyway. Charles could never be anything
but an ambassador, of course—I'd rather like that,
though they say it's stuffy. But there are other
things. Oh, dear, Garry, I've never talked like this
to anybody. I wonder why it is."

"It goes back a long way," I said, and we both
were silent. For I knew, or thought I knew, that
she had been talking, at the end, to keep something
away. While we talked of power and rule, it would
stay away, but there might be a time when we
would forget to talk. The doll's music hummed in
my head. I thought of the four Italian brothers
who had come to seek their fortune and found a
grave instead. But the memory helped us little,
for we were still struggling.

She flung her head back, in the gesture I remembered.

"Oh, so many people are dead!" she said. "And

[*141*]

so many don't care about living, except to be safe. I don't always want to be safe. It isn't enough."

Her face changed, and the mask came back, but I knew that something was altered. And when I saw the Obenheim sisters, that afternoon, they found me less punctilious than usual. I got practically all the Ingres drawings out of them and arranged to see the country house the following week.

The doll's music hummed in my head as I labored over the bargains, and Violet and I fenced when we met, with each other, and in the high rooms of the hotel James Shore was dying. He did not behave as if he were dying, he behaved as if he were withdrawing from life, as he might have from a faulty company, without rancor or concern.

Some of it was the lethargy of the disease, but I still think that some of it was chosen. He would sit on the balcony of his room for hours, smoking and looking at the garden. And, during that time, the books were always arriving from London or New York—the complete works of Swedenborg, in full morocco—the turgid rant of Brann the iconoclast—Gibbon and Winwood Reade and

Herbert Spencer—even Browning and Tennyson and *The Golden Bough*. But once the books were out of their cases, they would lie unread by his chair. "I used to be quite a reader, as a boy," he said to me. "But I guess you get out of the habit." Nevertheless he seemed to draw some sustenance from their actual possession. He had them all under contract, so to speak, from Plato to Brann, and, any time he chose, they would rise and deliver the goods.

Now and then he would have Miss Sunding read to him, but it was always one of two things, *Sam Slick the Clockmaker* or the cloak-and-sword romances of Stanley Weyman and his followers. I listened to *Sam Slick* once and found it very flat cider though with an unmistakable Yankee tang. But he never tired of it and would chuckle over the wooden-nutmeg jokes as easily the dozenth time as the first. As for the romances, he liked them best when they were the least like life. I tried him on *Vanity Fair*, but he could not get past the first chapters. "Too much about women," he said. The rest of the time, he would play Canfield endlessly, keeping an elaborate score in a leather notebook. Even so, he would think or gaze in the inter-

vals of the cards, and it would take him a long time
to play a game.

It was strange but not in the least pathetic.
It was evident that he did not know how to die—
but he was willing to learn. It sounds ridiculous to
say so—but you felt he was giving death a fair
trial. If it didn't suit him, he would stop and go
back to his business. He had no more faith in
doctors than he had in immortality, but he was
an excellent patient and followed all orders pains-
takingly. I could remember that he had done me
a wrong, but I could not hate him at all.

For I saw, without his telling me, that the wrong
had been automatic. He had separated Violet and
myself as he might two cards in a game of patience.
If the cards had fallen differently, he would have
played them another way. It was a game and you
played it as well as you could, without giving or
expecting justice. When you were tired of injustice,
you were tired of the game.

It amused him to see priests and ministers of
the Gospel, but the little priest from the Tyrol was
the one he liked, for he too was a player of a game.
In the eyes of the Church, James Shore's soul had
a value. James Shore did not believe he had a soul,

but he was used to dealing in values. They would fence for hours, while Allan Barker translated, his eyes growing larger and larger behind his spectacles.

"That man," said the little priest, cheerfully, "I have seldom met a more stubborn and obstinate heretic. But he is good for the wits. I have not quoted so much from the Fathers since I left the seminary." I do not think he ever really hoped to convert James Shore, but it was his duty to try, and the mercies of God were infinite.

As for James Shore, he made no promises at all. But he rather liked the arbitrariness of Catholic dogma. "You can't believe it, of course," he said. "But you can believe it a lot easier than that God's a Sunday School teacher. And it makes you feel kind of important. I was reading in some Indian book or other that you ought to spend the first fifteen years of your growth in making love, and the next fifteen in fighting, and the last in meditation. Well, I guess they grow up earlier in those hot climates. But there's something in it, all the same. I never took much stock in meditation, but it seems to come easier now. Or maybe I don't really meditate. Well, Colonel, how's business today?"

He tried to find out, as a game, just how business was with me, always, by what I said and didn't say. And when he got it wrong, as he did, he was quite amused. Amused and once, at least, a little disturbed. For he looked at me keenly and said, "How old are you, Grant?"

"Oh," I said, "about thirty-five."

"H'm," he said. "About Aleck's age. Well, a man ought to have a start in life by the time he's thirty-five. At least, I used to think so." He moved his head restlessly. "I wouldn't have picked you for it!" he burst out. "Well, you can't tell, all the time."

It was the closest he ever came to either apology or explanation, and it made me feel bitter. It sent me to Violet, somehow, and we talked more intimately than we had yet. It began casually enough, as those things do. And then she was suddenly saying, "Oh, I'm not blaming Charles. I'm not blaming any of the Mortons. But you have to come up for air."

She looked almost vulgar as she spoke, but it was the vulgarity of life that has to rule and be hindered.

"They're very fine people," she said. "But they

shouldn't have married me. Because now I have to stay with them. And I won't be like Aleck—I won't go to pieces. I'll end up being their ruler, if I live long enough. I suppose that's what Father wanted. But he should have given me a railroad."

She was in earnest now and rather terrifying. And I caught glimpses, through what she said of the secret battle, obscurely carried on, in the endless cycle of travel between one great house and one good climate and another that the rich pursue like birds. The Shores only battled for one thing, and that was power.

"All the same, I've been very lucky," she said. "I could have divorced Charles three years ago, the time I saw you in Rome. I didn't and I was right."

"In heaven's name, why?" I said.

"Oh, you never liked Charles," she said. "But that's not the point. I've given too much already. I'm not going to marry again and again like the rest of them. Charles is disloyal, but he isn't disloyal for long. The worst is his being pathetic, afterwards."

"I'm very sorry," I said, and, at the time, it was true.

"Oh, you needn't be sorry," she said, and her eyes were James Shore's. "I suppose we were all brought up wrong—even you, Garry. But there's no use being sorry for that. Only it was curious, seeing you, just then."

I did not deny it again, for I knew those images we make out of nothing. But I had not expected them in her, and it moved me, unbearably. I took her hands for a moment, and there was fate in the touch. Surely we could not hurt each other now.

"Don't think of it," I said. "This is different. This is new."

"I'm trying to think of it that way," she said, and we stood silent for a moment. Then we laughed rather falsely and talked about something else. But we had gone very far across the bridge of ice.

I do not know if James Shore watched us, and, if he did, I do not know what he thought. In any case, he said nothing. There was always that understanding between them as if they were both made of the same metal in a world of other metals. But she was a woman—and them he did not claim to understand. And perhaps he had come to a point in his meditation where certain problems of human life seemed meaningless to him. Again, I do not

[*148*]

know. I know that he disliked his son-in-law, though he never said a word against him. His grandchildren he was fond of, in a dry way, but with none of the sentimentality of certain old men. Their pictures were in his room, and he would look at them. But it was the look of a man who sees and is pleased with a pair of healthy puppies. Aleck's boy by the first marriage looked more like him than the others. But the mouth was not the same.

I commented on it once, and he said, "Well, Violet claims there's a likeness. But *her* family don't think so, and I guess you can't blame them. I won't say it was all Aleck's fault; because she was a featherhead. But I guess they're both better off the way they are, though I don't hold much with divorce. They say this one's clever—anyhow she's red-headed, and she's been married before. She's got Aleck started in fox-hunting, at any rate. And he looks well, on a horse."

He turned the conversation, and we talked of other things—of Harriman and Morgan and Gary, the railroads and the copper, the money and the steel. And, finally, we talked about money itself and what was to be done with it.

[*149*]

"It's funny," he said, "seeing all the people start running around with their little whitewash pots as soon as they begin to get old. Not that Jay Gould ever did. But a lot of the rest of them. So I guess I better have mine. Only nobody can put a brush in it till I'm dead."

"Who's going to use the whitewash?" I said.

"Oh," he said, "it'll be a foundation. That's what they're calling them now. What's that Greek word—means about life?"

I made a long guess. "Biology?" I said.

He nodded. "Uh-huh. Biology. I don't know much about it, but it sounds reasonable." It was exactly the tone in which he had said, "We've got money to pay for them now," when I was a child. "I had quite a few things looked up and, naturally, you're pestered a good deal anyway. But I've settled on that. I thought a good deal about just plain doctors, but John D. got in ahead. Well, I don't mean to copy John D.," and he smiled his dusty smile.

"I suppose they'll cut up frogs," he said. "Or maybe they've got past that, now. Anyhow, it'll be the James Shore Foundation." He pondered. "It wasn't Mary's being delicate," he said—it was

[*150*]

the first time I had ever heard him speak of Violet's mother directly. "She looked strong enough. But they didn't know so much then. You ought to know about the whole thing, not just sickness—that's the point. All the same," he ended, unexpectedly, "if Violet had been the boy, I wouldn't have done it. You like to keep those things solid. But she'll have enough."

He looked out over the garden again, and his eyes had a bleak wit.

"I thought of all sorts of things when I first started out," he said. "But I never thought they'd cut up frogs for me after I was dead. Seems kind of heathen, doesn't it? I guess I'll have some fun out of that with Father Pfefferlein."

It was that afternoon that Allan Barker button-holed me and asked me my honest opinion about the Big Chief's health. Certain reports had come in, and the Chief had hardly looked at them. "If it's anything much, they'll cable," he had said—and Barker was, obviously, as shocked as if he had refused a sacrament. But I knew instead, and suddenly, that his trial of dying had been a successful one and that he meant to go on, though I didn't say so to Barker. There was no use in

[*151*]

troubling that brisk emptiness with unnecessary realities. I let it appear that gods had their own divine and peculiar ways of functioning, and he went away quite satisfied. And, next day, James Shore seemed better and I was sure I was wrong.

It is not the words that make things definite, it is something else. We talked, that morning, by the tomb of the four Italians, and I think we both knew then, though we did not say so. When I opened the door of the apartment that afternoon to let her pass through, my mind was empty of anything but the smallest, most trivial things. There was wine and cake on the table—for a moment I hated their being there—I hated the discretion of the paid and rosy-faced servant who had understood so well what I had not said. It was a pleasant enough apartment, though very German— it was fortunate that I had taken it for the summer instead of staying at a hotel, when I found out the Obenheim business was likely to drag along. I hated the fortune and the discretion and the curtains drawn at the windows, though it was only afternoon. Then these things did not matter, because she was there, as I had seen her, with shut eyes, through the painful darkness, many times, when it was impossible, and in the bare rooms of youth.

We talked gayly and emptily for a few minutes, like actors who know their parts and their cues but are not yet convinced of the play. Then I went out of the room to get whatever it was that I was supposed to show her—a drawing, I think. When I came back, she had put her hat on a table and was lying back in a chair with her eyes half closed.

"I'm very thirsty, Garry," she said, without turning or moving. "Could you get me some water?"

I brought her some in a thick china cup, not a wineglass, and she drank it and thanked me. Then I put my hands on her shoulders. I knew it had to happen so, and I was quite calm, except for the beating of my heart.

"Ah, Garry," she said, after a moment, and a shudder passed over her body, like a small wave breaking.

It was so we betrayed each other, for comfort and delight and vengeance. For I knew well enough that it was not me she lay with but another than Charles Morton, and I knew well enough that I did not lie with her but with Charles Morton's wife. I remember the high German bed and all the cool, quiet stuffiness of the little room—I remember her shoes on the floor and a long slant of light through a crack in the curtains, almost touching them—I remember many small things, but I do not remember delight. That delight is over too soon, and we cannot live on its memory. Only the spirit can live.

Afterwards we were very civil with each other and a little shy. She turned her head away as she drew on her stockings, and I looked at my collar as if it were some strange species of shell. It was not shame or regret, but we suddenly knew we were naked and wished to be clothed. "It's outside us, really," said Violet, later, with one of her flashes of comprehension—and that was true. Our lives had diverged too far. We could stand beneath the cataract till our ears grew deaf with the sound, but we could not be united. But we said the words.

I think Dicky de Saugres would have laughed at our solemnity, and indeed, in certain moods, I was ready to laugh at it myself. We did our best to think of our love as a gay amusing interlude between two civilized people, and, now and then, we could talk quite like a play. But it wasn't so and we knew it. We could be letter-perfect in the easy lines, but our voices would betray us still— the barbarian voices, under the Roman accent, remembering, in ecstasy or anguish, neither Jove nor Venus, but the gods of desert and forest, the gods called Wind and Knife.

Once she said, without the slightest cruelty, "If you hadn't kissed me, that time, I mightn't have married Charles."

"And what am I supposed to say to that?" I said.

She thought for a moment. Then she laughed, dutifully.

"Yes, it does sound absurd. But I was thinking I wouldn't get married at all. I didn't like the idea. But then I knew I'd have to."

"Good God!" I said. "Weren't you in love with him?"

"Why, of course I was," she said, rather indignantly. "As much as I could be."

"How much are you in love with me?"

"I don't know. A great deal. But that's different. It always has been different, with you and me, Garry."

"How different? Tell me!"

[*155*]

"*Il ne faut pas jouer avec la serrure,*" she said, with a slight smile. "*Il est dangereux de se pencher en dehors.*"

Once she said, lying in my arms, "Is it all you wanted, Garry?"

"All," I said. "So much more than all," though I lied and knew that I lied.

"Then I've done that," she said. "That's something." She stirred. "Don't love me," she said. "Not now, not for a moment. After you'd gone, the first time, when I was alone and Aleck was cross, I used to play, sometimes—I'd go back to the cabin and you'd be there anyway. Only I couldn't make you move or speak because I couldn't invent that. But at night we'd both be asleep, and it would snow and snow and I'd wake up and hear it and then go to sleep again. I'd like it to be like that once." She lay with closed eyes. Then she smiled, and the smile was too wise. "But I know we're here," she said.

That was one of the few times we talked of the past, except with gayety, and of the future we hardly talked at all. Oh, I begged her to divorce Charles Morton and marry me, but, even as I begged, I knew I was unconvincing. It was part of the play, somehow, and the right words would not come. When she bloomed, and she did bloom in those few weeks, like a watered vine, I was dazzled but I was not proud. She had always been wasteful with her beauty, though not from humility. She could give it as free as air or light, she could use it like any of the tools of power, but I knew she did not think it important. And then, occasionally, I would have moods I had thought forgotten with first youth. I would look at her strong body and feel lonely, because it was made for great men. And there were only men like Charles Morton and myself.

Once she said, with that humorless directness that was as much a part of her as any of the things I loved, "I wonder what our children would have been like if we'd married, Garry."

"Bad painters," I said, and we laughed. And yet, later on, I found myself beseeching her like an imbecile or a eugenic congress. I cannot think of my arguments now without embarrassment, but they did not seem foolish then. Somehow I felt that such a child would defy all laws of heredity. It would take the best from both of us and be complete. I had wild dreams about it—with money

[157]

and cleverness anything could be done. We could hide it, like a child in a legend, in the high mountain valleys, and it would always be ours. And, oddly enough, she came nearer to accepting that than she did to divorcing Charles Morton. It would have been a result, and she did not value actions that had no results but themselves.

But "Oh, Garry, you're impossible," she said at last. "It would take nine months. And, besides, it wouldn't be fair." And, for that moment, I wished I were a rider, in the youth of the world, to take her in the short grass of a summer valley and give her a child whether she wished it or not. But the moment passed, and the next time I was only a man in trousers who put his watch on the table before he went to his desire.

Oh, yes, I was like Charles Morton at times, for we are all like that. And she was like every woman. But that is not to be helped. So many of the words are always the same. And yet it did not do ill to us. It would have been easy to sink, but we did not sink. It was there our solemnity saved us. She was many things, but she was not a light woman. Those who live and die by power can deceive and betray, but not, in these matters, lightly.

[*158*]

I could not think of her as a mistress, and when I was called to Paris to settle the Chalfont tapestries, we did not say good-bye as mistress and lover. I knew those scenes and those strainings—I was glad they were not for us. The Chalfont affair was a big thing, and I knew it; it wasn't so much the money, though that was important—but it put us definitely with the few very great dealers. For five days I worked as I had never worked in my life— and we brought it off. It took work, too, for Jules Guimard and Richards had almost muddled it between them—it wasn't Richards's sort of thing, and Jules Guimard lacked bluff.

When it was over, and the check deposited, Richards looked at me sourly.

"Christ!" he said. "How you can do it! I suppose there's an unknown Velasquez in the Obenheim ragbag, going for tuppence ha'penny!"

"No," I said, "just a Greco—a small one. Needs a little cleaning. Portrait. It seems to be a Bishop Sobolla—will you look up any possible history, Richards?—thanks. Von Eckholtz will fight it because it isn't in his list, but he won't fight after he sees it. He can't."

"Christ!" said Richards again, in a different

[*159*]

voice. "What period is it? When can I see it? Jules can't have it first—I want it. We won't show anything else for a year—I'll shut up the other rooms."

"As a matter of fact," I said, "we may not sell for five years. It might be wiser. Unless the Louvre or the Metropolitan—well. But Grecos are going up, all the time, and I suspect they'll keep on. Well, we'll see."

"Going up!" said Richards in a strangled voice. "A Greco Von Eckholtz doesn't know about! A brand-new planet! And you have the colossal, the incredible arrogance to say that the market—the market!—is going up and it might be a good stroke of business to——" He choked

"Oh, don't be an ass," I said. "You can have almost anything you like, next autumn. Except your Lithuanian friend who sculps women looking like milk bottles. I bar him. But anything else in reason. If we had a retrospective of Sir Edwin Landseer, it would go, after this."

"I wouldn't be surprised if you meant it!" said Richards, with a glare. "Not one bit sur——"

"*Sérieusement*," said Jules Guimard, pacifically —he never got accustomed to the rows between

Richards and myself—"*je crois que Sir Landseer est un peu vieux jeu. C'est seulement mon avis, vous savez, mais——*"

Then he stopped, for he saw that we were both laughing—we couldn't help it. He looked a little hurt at first, but after a moment, though with difficulty, he began to smile himself.

I remember the dinner of victory we had that evening—it was pleasant, though Richards and Jules were always an odd combination. The wine went to Richards's head and he called me a blood-sucking leech who fattened on the corpse of Art and remarked that I would be going into Society next. He described, with brilliant indecency, my nuptials with the daughter of a Press Lord, while Jules Guimard tried very hard to follow the conversation, with an expression of fixed but painful reproof on his face. Then Richards fell into a solemn mood.

"The trouble with you Grant is—" he said, and hiccupped gravely—"the thing about you is— you think you're a bloody adventurer and you're a bloody sentimentalist. You think you're bloody hard, but you've got a bloody soft spot somewhere. Oh, I don't know where it is, but it's bloody well got to be there. And some day, the two bloody things are bloody well going to pull you apart. So three bloody cheers for Van Gogh and to hell with all bloody art dealers!" Then he put his chin on his hands and started crooning one of the extraordinary collection of gutter-French ballads he had learned during his eight months' starvation in Paris, before he had given up trying to paint. I got him back to his hotel, finally, assisted by a scandalized Guimard.

"*C'est un type*," said Guimard correctly, after we had seen him to bed. "*Je n'aime pas ces types—là. Mais, je vous assure, que je ferai mon possible——*" and he shrugged. The shrug and a certain tone in his voice told me a great deal. They meant I was *le patron* now, and decisively. He would tell his uncle that *le patron* was mad, quite frequently, and they would discuss me at length, in the villa at Meudon, but he would follow me blindfold in spite of all that. I had the things in my hands, now.

I had the things in my hands—I had what I had worked for—and yet it didn't seem real. They hadn't bought Father's pictures—they would buy the ones I chose to sell from now on. Next year we would start in New York. And yet it wasn't enough. There was James Shore's daughter still, and something we hadn't found.

I wrote Violet a decorous note that anybody could read and resolved to take the roundabout route back, by way of Anderesplatz. I had not gone there before, in spite of my intentions—I had not wanted to meet the interest in my brother's eyes. But now, I thought, I would go and it would be good. I told myself I wanted to think.

It was August, and the brief Alpine summer was in the mountains. The snow was still on the peaks, but the air was changed. I was glad to walk beside my brother, glad we were men. He was gaining again, and Herz was fairly satisfied with him, though Herz seemed to blame me for the relapse. Well, that too had been a choice—and Carlo had had five free years. And I was glad to see Herz, too, in spite of his foibles. He had eyes as tired and keen as a watchmaker's, a long beard he combed with a little silver pocket comb, a gusty voice, and, behind it all, the passionate arrogance of the megalomaniac. But he was a great doctor, and I could trust Carlo with him.

Carlo knew, by now, that he never could be an

[*163*]

engineer, and it changed him, though he seldom talked about it. Once he did say, without any of the gestures of bitterness, "I'll have to write, I suppose. It seems to go with the disease. And you can do it on your back, if you have to."

"Well," I said, trying to be light, "they say it's a beautiful thing to be an artist."

"Oh, yes," he said. "And what would we do, without beauty? Just live and have a good time." He frowned. "It ought to be like building a bridge," he said. "Then it would be all right. But I wanted to build another kind. Of course I might have done it badly, though M'Quarrie seemed to think I'd learn. 'Ye'll have the rudiments in ten years or so, Mr. Grant.' But I expect Mother's right—the stain gets into your bones."

I knew what he was talking about and fell silent —there had been a paragraph in *Edelweiss* about the Infant Soul at the Gates and how ladies in long blue garments came and marked it with some sort of heavenly tattooing so that, when it emerged upon the world, it had to be an artist whether it wanted to or not. Carlo dropped the subject, but I had seen the first of the short prose sketches a year and a half before, when he had come back from the world. They were curiously bald and not at all clever, but they had an impact upon your mind—the impact of the hard stream of water you cannot cut with a sword. They were mostly the fruit of his five free years, and very few were concerned with Anderesplatz except the ones called *Temperature* and *Three Weeks More*. But when I showed Herz *Three Weeks More* he had said "*Ja*, that is the disease itself. It might have been written by the tissues. But your brother must not write any more like that. It does not matter at Anderesplatz, but it is not good at all for the people below."

I'd told Carlo that, and he'd laughed, though he was very weak. Now he had more sketches, enough for another volume, and I read them. They were the first of the American stories, and, when I read them, I knew that something had happened. If he could live, nothing would be wasted. I told him certain things, clumsily, and he laughed and said:

"Oh, I'll live, all right. But I would have died long ago if I hadn't had a brother. Yes, that is true, Garry. But I will not put you in a story, because I like you too much. Did I tell you I got a letter from the publisher? He says they have sold forty-two copies of *Three Weeks More* in six months, and it is not very much. Also that the British public has little interest in stories about Americans. But I am very happy, because my girl's temperature is down, and you are here."

It has always annoyed the critics, considering *Miss Waterbird* and *A Night At Prairie Sun*, that Carlo was never west of the Alleghenies, and they cannot understand it still. Well, Defoe was never on Juan Fernandez, but we have all been on that island and seen the marks on the sand. Even so, Carlo did what he did, and I have been told by professors that it made an appreciable difference to something called a "current" in something called "the literary scene." Not a great or important one, for, as they often point out to me, he died young, but still appreciable.

Whenever they say that, I see one of those marvelously sensitive scales that one finds in research laboratories. It is calibrated in ten-thousandths of milligrams and the very air can be sucked out of its glass case, like a spirit exorcised, so there shall be no mortal confusion at all. In one balance is a sliver of weight, so small it

[*166*]

must be handled with tweezers, and, in the other, a tiny crumb of steel. It took all Carlo's life and fifteen years of mine to make that crumb, and it weighs .003 of a milligram, according to the experts. Nevertheless, as far as they know, it is steel.

Iridium is rarer and platinum more valuable, but my brother's long body and his dark hair that grew as fast as a squirrel's, the shape of his skull and his sweat and the words he used in a different way from another man's, all the compact of thought and action and illusion, the intricate city, breathing lightly in sleep and in passion roused to one end, moving sometimes as if by itself and sometimes by command from a ruler, but never like another, never in all the days—all these made a crumb of steel to be weighed by tweezers. I do not find that unjust, but I still find it strange.

Meanwhile, it was pleasant to see him and talk to his girl. Her name was Lan, and she had the white Irish skin and a pretty voice. They were gay together, in spite of the illness—and it was not the gayety of fever—she was like Carlo in that. As soon as I saw them together, I knew there was nothing to do but be pleased with them, in spite of anything that might happen. They might die or live, but they were necessary to each other, and at ease. I was the healthy man, but my love and I were otherwise. It came upon me suddenly that my task with Carlo was done.

I tried to think it all out against the bare solidity of Anderesplatz, but it was hard to think in that changed, enchanting air. Only I knew this: I could play my part with Violet no longer, for what we did was empty. She must come to me forever or she must not come at all. We had done our best for gayety, but we were still barbarians. And I wondered if I wanted her to come.

There was a dark-haired English girl with her mother at the guest house in Anderesplatz. Her name was Caroline Vane, and they had come to see a distant cousin with a light case. It was a relief to be with her, for we had no common memories, only the present, and nothing to decide but whether we liked each other well enough to talk. I stayed on for three more days and flirted with her deliberately. She flirted charmingly, and we got on very well. I am not defending my conduct, I am merely stating what occurred. Carlo watched us a trifle puzzledly, but, on the whole, with approval. And then I went back to Vienna, full of plans and resolutions—and found that James Shore was dying.

It was not the disease which sent him to Europe that killed him, but pneumonia. He had gone out for a walk, as he did sometimes, and he had gone alone. A sudden shower had wet him through, and when he had hailed a carriage the driver had taken him back to the hotel by a roundabout route. It was Miss Sunding's afternoon out, and both Barker and Violet had supposed him to be in his room, for he had told them he wanted to rest. It was a very small contretemps, but it served to kill him. And yet he did not die easily, for, at the last, the strength of the flesh revolted and wished to live. But it could not any more.

I did not know that it was the end of an epoch, I thought it merely the death of a man. The hospital was already besieged with reporters, when I got there, and the cable wires were waiting. I remember talking to Barker, for a moment, and thinking that all his life he would tell people about this week. Violet came out with a drawn face and we said things. We could say nothing real because Barker was there. I offered any help I could, but

[*169*]

there was no help to be given. It had all been arranged, from the oxygen tanks to the cables to Charles Morton and Aleck. There was an efficient excitement in the hospital, like that of a great ceremony. One almost forgot that a man could die at all when everything was so efficiently arranged.

Nevertheless I saw him once and heard the hard, rough breathing. Now and then he would mutter, and Miss Sunding would wipe his lips. I heard a mutter as if he were dictating a letter, and a woman's name that sounded like "Estelle." His whole body seemed intent on the difficult business of breathing, but the dusty patience had not left his eyes. They were thoughtful and a little scornful in the dry mask of his face. Then he said, quite clearly and in a much younger voice, "I'll be damned if I do. They can take it or leave it. My name's Jim Shore and I'm running this." They put the oxygen mask over his face, as if to shut out the words. Then I was touched on the shoulder and hurried from the room.

He died the next morning, at the hour when so many die. The market broke badly at the opening but was given support and rallied in the afternoon. The papers began to explain that for some time

James Shore had gradually withdrawn from the active control of his affairs.

I had seen that withdrawal with my own eyes, and the reasons were not in the papers. They were within him. And I knew now that I had always hoped for a single phrase from him—a casual sentence that would explain him completely, that might explain us all. But he was not that sort of man, and there were no last words.

When the American newspapers came in, I read what they had to say of him. There were names and dates and anecdotes and the use of words like "titan." It was the American story and well handled. But he was more secret than that. I shall never know the secret, though I have made money, too.

We parted as we had met, his daughter and I, hastily, among crowds, at a station. It was better so, and we knew it. There was neither room nor decency for love in that publicity of death. There were too many eyes, too many cables and telegrams. Nevertheless we had thirty minutes to ourselves, the day before she left.

She walked up and down the room restlessly, in the black dress. I knew better than to put my hand on her or try and comfort her. I felt very tired.

She said, "I always knew there was something you couldn't beat. But I didn't know it was death. I should have gone into his room to see if he was resting. But there's no use thinking of that."

"After a while, it stops," I said.

"Oh, I know. I don't really think it. I'm tired, I suppose. There were people all day. But I don't want to sit down. I can hardly remember Mother . . . going into the room with Aleck when I was little and they were both there."

She pushed her hair back impatiently.

"Aleck should have been here," she said. "It doesn't matter about Charles. Anyhow, he offered to come. But Aleck should have been here. Just married or not."

She laughed sharply, and I thought she was going to go on. But she stopped.

"Just married," she said. "Just married. Well, I was here."

"Violet!" I said.

"I know, Garry," she said, quite quietly. "We were wrong, that's all. I expect we'll be punished for it."

"Nonsense!" I said, roughly.

"Oh, not by God or churches," she said. "And I'm not like Charles, I'm not afraid of the servants. But we pretended a lot. And now I can't feel it, any more. Tell me the truth, Garry, would you marry me tomorrow, if you could?"

I hesitated for the fatal second, and she saw it. All the time we had played our play, I had not thought of her as rich or poor. But with James Shore's death, it lay between us again, the money and the power. There were Dicky and his countess —like a caricature of what might happen, with the years. It would have been different, while I was still Rudolf Rassendyl. But we had both gone beyond that—and I had my own scheme of power, now. I knew, as I looked at her, that power is a heady thing.

"I'll tell you that in America," I said.

"Just so," she said. "If you ever come to America." There was neither defeat nor irony in her voice. "I don't know what there is between us, but we haven't found it yet. Now don't say 'we could try' or anything like that."

"I wasn't going to," I said, and, astonishingly, I felt suddenly at ease. This was neither my goddess

[*173*]

nor my mistress, but my fellow, the person who would be somewhere in my mind no matter what failed. And she changed, too, she relaxed, and the tension went out of her voice.

"I like you so much more than anyone," she said. "We couldn't have changed it, could we? But that stays."

"It always will," I said. Then we talked about little things, and the time was gone. And, as we talked, I knew that with James Shore's death she had fully become his heir. She would go back and rule the Mortons, not because she loved or did not but because she must rule or perish. And I would go on with my life and the self that I did not know. In the corridor, as I left, I passed Elsa Sunding, and stopped to say a few words. As I said them, I knew, somehow, that she knew about us, but I was not in the least afraid, for she too was secret. I was glad that Violet was taking her back.

I saw them again at the station, but merely to speak to. The officials had done their best, and they went to the compartment at once. The maid carried the same small bag, Allan Barker had on a black tie instead of a green. They would be met in Paris, they would be met in New York. Down the train the long box that is shaped like no other box was lifted into the car. James Shore was going back to America. He would pass through the mountains and the towns and the foreign city, swiftly, as he had done in life, with his secretary still at heel. When the train had gone, I thought of him in the train and then in the hold of the liner, deep down, deep down as the engines and the grimed men who fed the coal to them and slept like tired dogs on steel. He had driven many such men. Above, in the first-class dining saloon, the fresh flowers would be in the vases on the little tables, the bare-armed women dining, the stewards busy and servile. That, too, he had seen and measured with his arid eyes. James Shore was going back to America. They should bury him at Gun-flint, in one of the shafts of the mine, but they would not.

I left the station and walked slowly back to my apartment. There was always that cool stuffiness when you first went in. I went through each room in order, as a dog does, when people have gone away. But I did not expect to find anything. I came back to the salon at last and stood by the chair she had taken, when she first came there.

There was a great deal to be done, both with Richards and Jules Guimard, but I was not thinking of them or of the Greco. I was thinking that I had not heard music or walked till my bones ached or slept with no wish but sleep, in a long time. Perhaps these things are better with love, but that is not why I thought of them.

Something had been released, though it was not happiness. It had nothing to do with Violet, and yet it was because of her. I went out to the kitchen and found the thick cup she had drunk from and turned it, for a moment, in my hands. Then I let it drop and shatter on the red tiles, not in despair or anger, but because it was not fitting that anyone should drink from it again.

PART IV

I WENT to Anderesplatz again in the March of 1919. The train was old, cold, and grimy—it went wearily up the grades. I felt ill at ease in civilian clothes, ill at ease with peace. The soldiers had come home, but the world I had known was dead.

There have been books enough about the death of that world, and I do not intend to write another one. I know how hot and beautiful that August was in England—I remember the shape of the placards and the big words on them—the crowds in the streets—the talk, the courage, the bewilder-

ment, the tenseness, the maps and the colored pins.
I remember how long it took us to realize that
the world was over. Even on leave, quite often,
we would think we were going back.

Now the leaves and the war were ended and I
was tired. There had been certain people I had
worked with or known, but they all mixed together,
thinking. So many of them belonged to the other
world, the world that had still existed when I
married Caroline Vane. I could remember our
wedding day very clearly, and the clouds over
Archester spire as we left the church and the bells
rang. Enid had been there—a ruddy and altered
Enid, more English than the English—and Caroline's two brothers, who were killed on the Somme,
and Richards and Sir Hugo Isaacstein and some
old suitor of Caroline's whose name I couldn't
remember—Fossett? Faucit?—he played cricket
for the county and hated me and was tall. His
name didn't really matter, for he had died at
Gallipoli, but I should like to remember it. Caroline
hadn't meant to hurt him, but she had asked him
to the wedding because she was in love. She had
been in love with me when we were married. Yes,
that was quite true.

Mother had been magnificent, in purple, at the wedding. She had given Richards a presentation copy of *A Jaunty Heart In Art Land*, for, as she remarked, they were both Bohemians under the skin—and the coronets on her luggage had impressed Mrs. Vane. And Guido had kissed me on both cheeks, while his own were wet with tears. I could see him still, walking about the lawn in front of the parsonage in his narrow Italian shoes with one of Caroline's brothers beside him, entirely at ease and yet entirely un-English, while Caroline's brother bent upon him the fascinated gaze he would have given a macaw. The scene was small, unreal, and brightly colored, like something seen through the wrong end of a telescope. But that was how most things were that one remembered from those days, now.

We'd been going to make—what was it Richards had called it?—"a bloody Trust out of Art." But Richards was dead and wouldn't talk any more. Even so, he hadn't quite understood. But we'd planned to open the New York gallery in October, 1914. It would have been a good show, especially the Parisinis. We'd got out of the lease all right— at a profit, for that matter. Perhaps we should have given our show anyway—but that had no importance any more.

There were pictures in cases and crates and pictures on the walls of rooms. There were a great many things in boxes and crates, and some of them were quite valuable and many of them fine. But I couldn't feel them any more. When I went back to my house, I had looked at the two Zamacoya drawings I got from Mannheim, and even they were gone. I knew what they were, but I wasn't interested in looking at them. There was an arrangement of lines on paper, but that was all.

I would have to start in again, yes. I would have to start in again, but how? With two years—three years more—we would have been solid. But the war had caught us in a stage of crystallization. It wasn't the individual losses that mattered, or the long stagnation. The great dealers, like Dyner's, would begin again, as soon as there was any dealing. But we'd made our name too rapidly. Yes, it was to do over again, and there might be no way to do it, for the combination was broken.

It meant nothing, beside what had happened to the world, and yet it was rather a pity. Sir Hugo Isaacstein had been very much interested. His beautiful, long-fingered hands had played with an ivory paperknife while he talked to me about the kingdoms of the earth. "Well, why not, Mr. Grant? It was the kings who patronized art first —then the merchants. I suppose they can say this will be the merchants, too—I am a merchant, of course—but there will be a certain difference. Yes, I think we can do something a little different. At any rate, I should be glad to try."

He had been a brilliant Jew, supple, melancholy, and daring. He had dreamed of Art as an integer of civilization, not an ornament—of a machine of Art which would make the simple things that all people use and make them beautifully and well. It wasn't to be Wardour Street or William Morris wallpapers—he wasn't that sort of man. Nor was it entirely a dream. He had spent his rare leisure on the project for ten years, and some of the details were extraordinarily practical. "The good form drives out the bad, Mr. Grant—if it's cheap enough—always if it's cheap enough."

Well, there was a set of cups and saucers on a shelf in the London house. Perhaps they were not as excellent as we had thought them, but they would not be made again—the designer was gone, with his sketches, and the potter blind. They

[*183*]

differed very little from the cheap cups sold on every counter—except that they were good instead of bad. We had started in a small way enough, but they had cost a great deal of money. We'd have got it back in the long run, but there hadn't been any long run.

We'd called the company Art Industries, Ltd. "Get an ugly name," said Sir Hugo. "Then they'll think you're practical. And nothing about peasants and folk dances, please." I wondered where all the plans were, the typewritten sheets and the notes in his small, curled hand. They would do me no good if I had them, for they needed the brain that had made them to carry them through, but I wondered. I had talked to the heirs, but there was nothing to be done with them. They had not approved of Sir Hugo's remaining a Jew—it was something they were trying to escape from as rapidly as possible, with daughters named Shelagh and Rosemary and a grouse moor in Scotland. They'd thought I wanted my money back—but it hadn't been that. When we saw the cups we were pleased with them, that July.

That had been in the days when there was a great deal of time. There was time to get married

and make plans and buy the furniture for a house
—time to be very busy at Art Industries, Ltd., and
heckle Guimard and Richards and learn about
pottery and keep a dozen balls in the air at once—
for Carlo's book of stories was coming out and
one's wife was giving a dinner party and there was
lots in the papers about Suffrage and the Irish
business and the Greco was on special view.
There was time to be pettish and take baths and
feel a little abused at working so hard. Now there
was a great deal of time again, but it did not seem
the same.

I rubbed the frozen breath from the window of
my compartment and stared out at the bleak,
bright landscape, thinking of Caroline. I had
married because I wished to, but she had married,
hoping for love. I knew that now, entirely, when
it was too late to know. Her love had been like
the slow skies and the settled, fertile landscape—
something gentle and very natural—something to
be possessed in peace. There had been much time
but no peace. And then, for four years, there had
been neither peace nor time.

I took some comfort, thinking of Mrs. Vane.
Mrs. Vane had been a charming woman, but her

[*185*]

eyes were both hungry and bitter and she would have given her daughter to a worse man. And when I had taken her daughter, I had taken her with good intent. I had known love before, but never protection, never the wish to cherish. I had felt it, like a passion, in the first months of our marriage. But it had not been enough. It might have been enough, in time, for we were growing together. But then had come the shaking of the world.

It had not broken my wife or killed her or made her bitter. The change was more subtle than that. There are certain plants—if you move them to too strange a soil, they will grow, but they will not flower. I wondered when it was that she wakened and nothing in the room was changed but she knew that I was alien. I could think of it quite dispassionately, as if it had happened to another man and another woman. It had happened, in spite of forethought or good will or any plans.

She would always be loyal, but she had been frightened. And, out of her fear, she had built herself, slowly, impenetrable armor. She would not be hurt again, except through her children, and those she guarded defiantly. I could blame myself, if I liked, but the blame went beyond me as well. There was no one to blame for the collapse of Art Industries, Ltd., and the schemes that were to rise from it. Sir Hugo's two sons had been killed within a week of each other, that was all. They were nice boys, but neither of them had his father's brains. However, they happened to be what he lived for. He went on for a year after that, like a machine slowly running down.

I remembered the taste of whiskey and the smell of dressing stations. They mixed and were cold in my belly, but that was getting better. I was no longer Orderly Sergeant Grant, R.A.M.C., and a disk. It had seemed necessary to do that, after Caroline's second brother had been killed. It had been sensible of the British government to suspect me because I made visits to Switzerland to see my sick brother. Sensible but stupid. It had made things difficult. Still, Sir Hugo had been able to manage it—it had been in the days when he was still able. Later on, he had kept in touch with Carlo while he could. I owed him a great debt for that, and I would never be able to pay it. There were many facts of that sort, cold, hard, and un-dissolved, in my mind.

The taste of the mouthpiece of a gas mask came

suddenly, without premonition, and went. Major Archibald Herrington, D.S.O. Lance Corporal Albert Edward Slye. The Senegalese with the head wound. Names and faces. Sections of broken landscape. I changed the dressings. I heard the unmistakable click of the knife on bone. But it was only the train.

I remembered my first sight of American troops. They looked singularly big and young. As if they shouldn't be killed, they looked. But they were, of course, for I saw some of them later. They had good cigarettes, not like gaspers, and sometimes very sweet chocolate. But I was used to gaspers, though I liked the boy from Kansas City. He had run a gas station before, and we had trouble over that, explaining. "The American language is now diverging from English at many important points." It was wonderful how stupid sentences stuck in your mind. If my father had not diverged from the American language at several important points, I might be living at 4724 Rosebud Avenue, Kansas City. As it was, I was "C. of E." on an identification disk, and, on other papers, a loyal subject of King George.

It was stupid of Richards not to have had a bad

heart. He should have had a bad heart or bad eyes or conscientious scruples. Then he would probably be alive. But they'd found him perfectly sound and, naturally, they were correct. He was perfectly sound—it was merely evident in his looks and body that he was quite sure to be killed. Doubtless that could not be allowed for, in examining men for a war.

He had lasted eight months and written me some curious letters. The last was a very indignant one—he'd seen the review of a book on Chinese ceramics, and it infuriated him not to be able to get back and prove the author wrong. He was perfectly capable of deserting, in order to do it, but he hadn't. They'd hung the patrol on the wire. His uncle had come from Hornsey to talk to me—a pursy little man with a red face and bad teeth. "Pore Alf, 'e was always muckin' abaht wiv paints." Alfred Gladstone Richards—he always signed it A.G. I never knew he had an uncle. Where the devil, and from what ancestor, had he got the sensitive taste and the thirst to learn and the hands? It no longer mattered. We'd never thought of liking each other, but we had done work together and I missed him very much.

[*189*]

It was stupid of them to kill Dicky de Saugres. They should have let Dicky alone—there was no sense at all in killing him. It was one thing, and a worse one, to kill the good and the brave and the just. But to kill the gay and the trivial and the worthless—that broke something else in the mind. I'd seen him once, in 1915, and we'd shaken hands. He was perfectly brave, and he looked like a fox terrier caught in a bear trap. I had asked for the Countess de Saugres. "*Madame la Comtesse ne peut pas m'accompagner aux tranchées,*" he had said. "*C'est déjà quelquechose. Il faudrait, vraiment, une guerre mondiale pour ça.*" Then he'd smiled a little and shrugged. "*Quand nous reviendrons,*" he had said, "*nous serons tous vieux. Ça sera drôle— très drôle. Mais, moi, je n'ai jamais pris la vieillesse au sérieux.*" Well, he had not had to take his old age seriously or otherwise for he had not returned. Madame la Comtesse had been active in good works—I had seen her name as a patroness of various leagues. She would be secure from now on—in that new society of Rumanians, Greeks, and others that meant to run Paris—Dicky's death had made her secure.

It was stupid to live through the war and then nearly die of influenza. But one did stupid things.

I was quite well now. The train was really cold, but we were mounting, the air was clean. The brandy made warmth in my throat, and, as it did so, three walking cases came down from the Line, with the stare and the dirt on their faces. Then they also disappeared. They came so very much less often already; in the end, I supposed, they would seldom come. I would think about making money, for a while, because I would be met at Anderesplatz, and I did not much want to think of that. I had meant at one time, as I remembered it, to devote my life to my brother. But I had not seen him in more than two years, and he was dying now.

They had had a different wedding from ours, in the overupholstered front parlors of the sanatorium. There had been sweet champagne and speeches, and people had sung "O Tannebaum" for no particular reason. Somehow, it had been like the gala night on a small liner, with nearly everyone being rather friendly and silly. They were gay, even Herz and the Egyptian, because Carlo and his girl were gay. Herz made a very funny speech and imitated himself—I didn't think he had it in him. When the dancing began, I went whirling around the room with a Swedish girl who stamped her feet like a peasant, and across, I could see

Herz whirling solemnly, with his beard stuck out. I felt suddenly very happy—I was to be married myself in a couple of months. Then I realized that Lan and Carlo had left the room, and with them the gayety.

He must have been very lonely after Lan died. Yet he lived and finished his book. The last letter I had from him concerned it. It was called *The Frozen Heart*. I'd have time to read now, time to think and talk. Plenty of time. Then it struck me like a blow where I was and why. I took some more brandy, not enough to make me drunk but enough to make me warm. Only the heart was not warmed, it stayed perfectly cold. Perhaps that was what Carlo meant—I should have to read his book. The train slowed, inexorably.

When I went into the room I wondered, automatically, where his wound was. I was used to men dying of wounds, and it seemed strange for any to die outside of war. Then I saw his face and forgot. It was more than the two years older and very thin. You could see the strong sculpture now. The eyes looked beyond me, not seeing me. They were quiet. It was the face of a man. He had done what he wanted, after all.

I kept seeing the other boy, unchildlike for a child. He had been charming enough, but there was always something besides. A little core of hardness, sharp as a crystal, that nothing could melt or taint. I had seen no one die, in peace, since James Shore died—and that seemed far away—but this was another death. The act itself was no different, nor the extremity of the body. But the face itself made me wonder. All my life I had thought of him as my younger brother. I would do so again, when he was dead, but I could not, now.

I felt nothing at all when the breath stopped, though I knew at once. I turned to the nurse.

"Don't stand there looking," I said, with a mechanical rasp in my voice. "Where's Orderly Harris? Don't you know they'll need the bed?"

She knew what to do for me, and she did it quickly. But it seemed a long time before the needle stung and I could go to sleep.

The ground was as hard as iron in the cemetery; they had to light a fire on the ground before they could dig the grave. I was quite empty of emotion, but the tears kept running out of my eyes. I was afraid they would freeze, as I stood there, and blinked continually. A part of my mind kept wondering what shell could make so small and neat a hole.

There were words and the coffin sank. I looked around for Herz, but he was not there. Then I remembered, of course. The sanatorium had been closed for three years and Carlo had died in the little house in the village my money had bought him. I had meant to do a great many things for my brother. I had bought him a house where he and his wife could die. For all that, they had liked the house.

I wondered if Herz was alive. I did not think so. It was very soon after the Armistice, but he would have come back to Anderesplatz, like a bee returning to its hive, if he had been able. He had been above wars, above the nations who make them— man himself had not interested him greatly, only life and death. Nevertheless he had gone. He had probably made a good field doctor. No, they would have done better with him than that—they were clever at using their men. It struck me suddenly that he had been a German, and I almost laughed. He had no nationality now. The tears had ceased to run from my eyes, but they lay on my cheeks like ice.

I stayed on, for three weeks, in the house I had bought for Carlo. Mother and Guido were there for five days; then they went back to Rome and I was alone. I telegraphed Caroline not to come— it would have been hard for her to leave the children, in any case. I am not the sort of person who goes mad, so I cannot say that the three weeks saved my reason. But they saved me from something, they enabled me to go on living.

I talked a great deal with Mother, even about the war. She knew a great deal more about it than I, for she had written *Italy, My Italy* and lectured all over America for the Italian Red Cross. But that did not hurt me. She was still remarkably vigorous, but her hands were the hands of an old woman. She and Guido took great care of each other—they were timid when the other sat in a draft. I suddenly realized that there was no one else to take care of them. There was no one because each, by now, by the mere process of life, had become irreplaceable to the other, not only as a person but a custom, an echo, a bundle of memories. For memory is the end and beginning, it outwears beauty and splendor, it endures beyond sympathy and wit. At the last we are glad to seek

[*195*]

out our oldest enemy and talk to him of the things that we both have known. And when he dies, a part of us dies with that death.

Most of all, I liked to hear Mother talk about her girlhood and the first few years of her married life. Often enough she talked like one of her books. But a phrase would come or a sentence, and I would suddenly see a girl I had never known, young, ardent, a little silly and quite courageous, sitting up late after a ball with her thick hair over her shoulders and her fingers getting inky, to copy Browning in her diary because of the blond young man with the artist's beard.

It must have surprised her young man to find her so steadfast for truth and Browning—it must have surprised her friends. Perhaps, in the end, it even surprised herself. Everybody knew pretty Kitty Antwerp and hoped she would marry money, though she was a fearful tease. "I always say I was spiritually born in Rome," said my mother, solemnly—and then Kitty Antwerp was gone, there was only Catherine Grant, Contessa di Capponegri and the author of many books. But I saw that Catherine Grant was satisfied with her life. After her initial revolt she had never faltered once but marched breast forward, the torch clasped firmly in her right hand. The torch had never really been lit, and the march, at times, had been over all of us, but, now that I was older, I recognized and saluted the indomitable and unpredictable persistence that had driven the marcher on.

We had been a clan, but we were scattered. Mother had seen Imogen in California. She showed me the photograph of the stout, unrecognizable woman, her eyes a little squinted with the fierce sun, beside the baldish man in the chaplain's uniform with the chaplain's official smile. There was a girl child between them, large, blonde, lymphatic, and flavorless. It seemed perfectly healthy, but it looked as if its veins ran spinach instead of blood. There was that child and Enid's four—the eldest had been blown to bits in the spring attack. There were Caroline's and mine. There were the houses and the husbands, the wives and the places in life. I wondered how we would look, if you got us all together again—if there would be any tie. Petrus Antwerp had crossed the sea to settle a wilderness, and Alexander Grant had had a conviction of grace. They had come to the new country in the sailing ships; it was a long voyage.

There were Doanes and Grants and Antwerps—and we, at the end. But the best of us was dead and had left no child—only books—only the terrible marks on paper that outlast life but never replace the dead.

I had not thought for a long time of a woman called Violet Shore. Only when they bombed the hospital the second time, and it was worse, being the second time. I thought of her now, without infidelity or longing. Her children were older than mine, soon the boy would be well grown. It seemed fantastic that we had ever been lovers—it seemed even more fantastic that she would be—what was it?—forty. Yes, she had been eight when I was ten. I wondered if there were grey in her hair. There was grey in Enid's, but Enid was older.

She would have been busy, these years. Men in Charles Morton's position did not actually go to war—but still they would have been busy. I wondered if the strong engine had crushed and stamped the metal of life as it wished. I did not think of her with love, for my heart was frozen, but I thought of her. Every day, when Mother and Guido had left, I took skis and went up as far as the empty sanatorium. It would reopen next year, I heard, under other management. The people of the village would be glad of that. But now it was quiet and the windows were blind. I did not mind the blindness—it was more peaceful, that way.

Then, one day I knew I must go back, for I was well enough. I stopped in Paris, for a business conference with the Guimards. They were glad to see me, but Jules was about to get married, and the old man had come out of his retirement to do what little could be done in the last four years. I suddenly knew that I couldn't do it again—that the curve was broken. Jules had sound ideas about a much smaller business—he could carry them out, but not with me. Besides, there was Caroline, and the children I barely knew. We talked for a day and a half, and then, unexpectedly, an American company offered us a premium for the remaining years of our lease on the Rue de La Boétie.

I could see that Jules was sorry and yet relieved when I accepted it—he had fought four years and wanted a quiet life. We came to an arrangement, and I retained a sleeping partner's interest in the new venture, but that was all. Jules had kept the beard he had grown in the war—already he looked like what he meant to become—the serious

[*199*]

antiquaire with a steady, profitable trade and a specialty. He had followed me once—he would have followed me still at demand—but he had never really thought me solid. Well, perhaps I was not—that was something I still had to find out.

I still do not like to think of the next few months, after my return to London. I tried very hard to be interested and to get things started again, but I seemed to have lost the touch. It was as if a slight but impermeable curtain hung between myself and the world. We reorganized the London gallery and began again, but I had forgotten the tricks of success. I had not been like Richards, but I had had a flair. Now the flair was gone, because, when I looked at the canvas and the wood and the cloth, the metal and the porcelain, they meant nothing to me, though I could still talk about them. The only real things left were the cups and saucers we had looked at that July—and they were no help, for they could neither be sold nor made again.

I wished to be very busy, and I was so. But you can be quite as busy ruining a business as you can in creating one—and, everywhere I turned, I made the wrong guess. There were others doing the same thing—I wondered, sometimes, how many of us there were, all over Europe. For there was a fever in Europe—the fever of the Peace—and it produced strange symptoms.

Between Caroline and myself there was a curious truce. I could not conceive that she liked the life we led, but she seemed to want no other. It was not an intimate life. We had a set of acquaintances and we went out a great deal. It was what is known as a cosmopolitan and artistic group—neither fish, flesh, nor herring. It gave parties and meddled with the Arts. They were the sort of people whom Carlo particularly detested—but Carlo was buried at Anderesplatz. They made noise, and the noise sounded cheerful, when there was enough whiskey in the glass.

A Nanny took care of the children, and with them, too, was Caroline, always watching. It made a wall. I was fond of my sons, but already their voices were different from mine. They were good children, healthy and pleasant, but we had little time together. I was always going to make time and never did.

I was always going to make time, but I had to make money. For money got to be more and more my excuse and my justification. If I could give

Caroline a great many things that she did not want, I could feel absolved. I encouraged her to be extravagant and rash and fantastic. And then, sometimes, at night, I would wake and wonder how long it could go on before the ultimate, shaming crash. It was a curious state of mind. The gambler knows he is going to lose, but he will steal or kill to get the money to lose. I could bear the essential separation between myself and my wife, but I could not bear giving up the rôle I had worn when I first met her—the alien adventurer who picked dollars out of the air.

I suppose I was really looking for self-pity, for I know, when I read it, I did not like *The Frozen Heart*. There is very little self-pity in that book, though the man who wrote it was ill enough. I arranged for its publication because it was Carlo's, but when Vallandigham comes back to his house after life has failed him, I stopped reading. There was something in the character that I did not want to see. I have read it since, with full knowledge and understanding, but that was later. Then, I turned away—to the men who talk in bars about great projects, the frank-eyed and hearty men who seldom turn honest pennies, the men with the secret mouths and charming manners who carry through large swindles and are often believed in to the end.

It was for some of those men that I went to America, in the end. I shan't go into the details of the project. We'd had a bad year, and it was a chance to recoup a little. But it was stuff I wouldn't have touched in our great days. It wasn't so bad, in itself, but I knew it was the thin end of a wedge. I had been a good many things, but not, so far, a tool, and we'd made a certain reputation. After this, we would begin to have a different sort of one. It wouldn't even be like Mannheim's—a consistent rascality—but something puffy and second-rate, like a boiled Brussels sprout, with the cabbagy taste of petty knavery about it.

Nevertheless I got a certain satisfaction out of dealing with my principals. They meant to milk the gallery, and I could still see that much, in spite of the curtain between myself and the world. I remembered Richards saying, "You think you're bloody hard—but you've got a bloody soft streak in you somewhere"—I wondered how they had known. And it rested me to be on the ship, to be free of all responsibility, to know there were five days, four days, three days, before I would land. I spent those days, cherishingly, doling them out. While they lasted, I was still, at least, my own man.

They ended. It seemed strange to see that high skyline again as a stranger. It seemed strange to see that flag and the statue with the torch. The tugs came, nuzzling the liner into dock. "There's Joe, there's *Joe!*" said a voice. Another said, "Well, God's country." It was here.

I did not remember the shadows in the streets— it had been, as I remembered it, an open city, full of quick sun. It did not seem to me as if the buildings had risen but as if the streets had sunken, as if some enormous, invisible pressure had chan- neled them deeper and deeper into the rock. I felt, that first day, as if there were a great weight on the island—as if I should step softly because of the weight. They had built something too high and too heavy for the ground.

Then the feeling passed, and with it came in- toxication—the intoxication of the clear dry sting- ing air. It was this that James Shore and his successors had built—this superb and barbarous splendor. They had done it without intention, and

[*204*]

there was nothing like it in the world. It was beyond vulgarity, for it was beyond belief. All other cities I had known had been places where people could live. But this was not a place where people could live—it was a triumphal shaft, pointed angrily at the sky and always rising—a shaft upon which the hard electric beam wrote inscriptions too swiftly for the eye.

The women walked richly in the streets—there were so few of them in black. Even the poor looked fed. Somewhere, I knew, there must be starving faces, but I did not see them. Somewhere there must be the cripples, the blinded, the gassed, but they were hidden away. A few men in worn army trench coats looked cold as they wandered the autumn streets—their eyes had no home and their cheeks were tired—but they were few, they were swallowed up in the torrent that poured in and out of office buildings and shops and picture palaces, the torrent of buyers and sellers, the faces of the advertisements, young, nervous, clean-shaven, massaged, pink with health and the cold.

Everywhere I went I saw Allan Barkers—the blue suit with the white pin stripe had almost become a uniform. There were so many alike, the

[*205*]

tall, admirably walking, silk-stockinged girls were pretty as a basket of apples and alike—the middle-aged men of affairs with the pink, chubby faces and the teeth that had eaten soft food might have been interchanged like parts in a standard machine. When they played golf, in their knickerbockers, they looked like a club of plump boys and they had the jokes, the loyalties, and the occasional sadness of boyhood in their play.

It was not all so, of course, and much of it was my mood. There were other faces, the subtle and the quiet—and the face of a man I saw in the middle of the five-o'clock torrent, an old man, lean, with dry cheeks and black clothes that were Sunday clothes. He belonged to another America, from the veins on the back of his hands to the sun wrinkles at the corners of his eyes. He was jostled by the crowd, but his eyes were reflective, not bewildered. But when the null, handsome face of the Republican nominee for President was cast hugely upon the screen of a picture palace that evening, and the darkness clapped, I felt, somehow, as if it were an apotheosis. Something had won, and it was not even a principle or a fear. It belonged to the new, smooth faces—I thought of James

Shore—I thought of the lucky prospectors and the man with the nose of a parrot—I wondered where the smooth faces had come from to supplant those faces of strong prey. They had roofed Park Avenue, they had put the trains underground.

Then I read that the Shore house in the Sixties was to be torn down. I felt a little dizzy when the newspapers spoke of it as a landmark. They opened it, for some charity or other, and, for three days, you could pay your fifty cents and walk in. I went in the last day—there wasn't much of a crowd. There was a kitchen table in the front hall, and a girl sat there with a box to take your money. She was dressed in a smart dark suit, and there were flowers on her coat. I had seen her a thousand times before, in pictures, in hotels, along the Avenue, and there was something about her nervous poise that reminded me of the lacquer and bright metal of a brand-new car. They turned so many out, they systematized it so well, the endless belt of production flowed without stopping. Pretty soon there would be cars and girls all over the world.

There was grime on the marble of the hall, and the imprint of rubber heels. The rooms looked big and gaunt with the furniture out of them—how could people ever have lived in such a comfortless place? The crowd wandered about rather aimlessly and silently, fingering the carvings on the fireplaces and staring solemnly at doorknobs and ceiling moldings and the marble bathtub upstairs. They were looking for splendor and arrogance and the traces of guilty revelry, and they did not find them.

"Say, it must have cost a lot!" they'd say, but their voices were disappointed. "Do you suppose that's real gold, on the ceiling?" said a thin woman, wistfully. "I guess it's just gold paint." "Well, all the same, I wouldn't want to live in it—it's too drafty." "Well, you just give me the chance!" and a laugh. I could see James Shore watching, with his dry smile. He hadn't particularly cared about it, either—it was one of the things you bought when you made your pile.

There was a little knot about the elevator where the hastily inked sign said "Not Running." "It's real old-fashioned," said a voice. The wreckers would come soon enough and take it all away. It had cost a great deal, but there was nothing in it worth saving except a couple of the fireplaces and the marble bathtub that looked like soiled yellow

[*208*]

stone. I had read in the papers that the walls were three feet thick in some places. The wreckers would have trouble with them. A hotel was to rise on the site. I wondered what would be worth saving when they came to wreck the hotel.

I was out in the kitchen, by now, staring as vacantly as the others at the great coal range that should have roasted whole oxen and never had. And then I saw a face across the room that I knew. I could not be mistaken in Elsa Sunding, though I had not seen her in eight years. I went over to her and spoke. She looked at me for a moment without recognition. Then she said, "Oh, yes, indeed, how do you do, Mr. Grant."

We made remarks about coincidences, and I asked her to tea. She glanced at her wrist watch. "That is very nice of you," she said, in her professional voice. "Yes, I will just have time."

We went to the Plaza. It was Saturday afternoon, and the dance floor was crowded with youth. I felt puzzled again, because even the youth seemed cut to one of two or three patterns, but they were good to look at. "Who are they?" I said. "They look as if they owned the world."

"Oh—boys from college—nice enough girls,"

said Elsa Sunding. "Yes, they do look like that, don't they? Well, you see, they've been told a good deal about themselves. They're a generation, you know." She smiled.

"Who isn't a generation?" I said.

Elsa Sunding smiled again. "You'd have to ask my boy," she said. "He's only fourteen, but he's read all the books. There are quite a few of them, mostly written by young people. They are very enthusiastic and disillusioned. He is looking forward to college, when he can be properly disillusioned himself."

"I beg your pardon," I said. "I've been calling you Miss Sunding."

"I have always been Mrs. Sunding," she said, quietly. "It does not matter." She looked around the room. "They dance after all the wars," she said. "But I am glad my boy will be older, when he goes to college." She looked at me directly. "Have you seen Mrs. Morton?" she said.

"No," I said. "I've only seen the house."

"I have seen a great deal of them," stated Mrs. Sunding. "There is always a great deal to be done, in a family such as that, and I am a trained secretary as well. I am with Miss Flower now."

"Good heavens!" I said. "I didn't realize that Aunt A—that Miss Flower was still alive!"

"Oh, yes," said Mrs. Sunding. "She is frail, of course. But she has her own apartment and is very comfortable. She could be in the country, but she does not like it in the country. She misses the other house when she remembers, but that is not often. That is why I went there today—the night nurse let her see the papers. We do not generally let her see the papers—they merely disturb her. However, now I have been there, she will believe me, and we can go back to our other reading. There is a book called *Little Daisy*. Did you ever read it?"

I sucked in my breath a little. "No," I said.

"It was a popular book when she was a child," said Elsa Sunding reflectively. Her composure broke for an instant. "Ah, rather to die in a ditch!" she said, deeply. "But it is unprofessional to discuss one's patients. You must excuse me." She smiled. She consulted her wrist watch. "I must go in ten minutes," she said.

There were many questions I had wished to ask her, but now I did not choose. I kept thinking, not of Violet, but of Amy Flower, the girl who had danced out her Eastern slipper soles on the last of the frontiers, the girl who had been caught by accident in the whirling, ascending spiral of James Shore's rise to power, with no defense but her woolwork and a certain meekness of mind. She had never comprehended the power, yet she had outlived James Shore. Now she was happy enough, when the papers did not disturb her. It seemed a strange life to have lived, though all lives were strange.

I wondered about the spiral, when Elsa Sunding had left me. It must continue to rise, for that was its nature. Already it had cast one house aside. I could see it, rising like the buildings, to some undreamed-of height. Only what would be at the top? It was hard to know.

I thought of another spiral—for I had been back to Maremmah. It had taken me a day that I should not have spared, but I was curious and Mother wished a photograph of the house for her reminiscences. Unfortunately, she would not be able to use it, when she got it, for it did not fit her description at all. The house was old enough, but neither quaint nor stately, and someone had added a porch that gave an unmistakable effect of false teeth. I didn't think Mother would care for a photograph of the brickworks, though I took one—they had passed through a dozen hands since Jared Antwerp's, and the present owners were only too anxious to sell. Still, there were a few old tiles and I'd brought one away with me— it wasn't really Jared's, but Guido would make a sketch of it and then it would be all right.

I asked, idly, if there were pottery clay in the neighborhood—oh, yes—they'd thought of starting up a kiln, once, but you couldn't compete with the big fellows. However—they had some samples left, if he could find them. He did so and I crumbled the stuff in my fingers—it wasn't bad clay. I thought of my cups and saucers in London, and dreamt, for a moment, absurdly. Then I knew it was absurd and asked the way to the graveyard. There was, actually, a half-effaced stone with Petrus Antwerp b. and d. April 17th, 1811. That was one of the half-great-uncles, who had died in childhood, while Jared was still making bricks, before the canal-boat frenzy and the greater fortune. I was only the fourth in descent from Jared, but it seemed a far cry. He and the first Charles Morton must have been nouveau-riche together—the thought rather pleased me. But we'd come to America before the Mortons, and Mother would be sure to point it out.

I wondered about the New Hampshire town where the first James Shore had settled—I wondered about the Methodist, Alexander Grant, and his conviction of grace. They were thoughts without conclusion, but Maremmah was a pleasant town. The big trees were still in the streets, and the historical societies had not found it yet. Indeed, there was nothing to find, for people had merely lived there and done nothing famous but live.

If the house had been the house of Mother's reminiscences, and all the graves standing beside one another, like a family group in a photograph, I would not have been stirred at all. But there was only Petrus Antwerp and the broad river below the town. They had gone on, leaving their dead. They must have buried the first Petrus on his farm, but I didn't have time to look for the place, before I went back to the station—the train connections were bad. To build a house in the wilderness—but then they had lost their way. What was it that they had lost? The town did not tell me, though the river was still there, as it had been when the banks were wilderness.

I had a sudden picture of my father, in his velvet-collared jacket, the jacket of an artist, working away at "Nero" while the sunlight poured through the windows of the foreign room. He had run away with Kitty Antwerp, he had meant to be a painter and yet a gentleman. He must have looked at the crowd of us with puzzled eyes. But I could reconstruct nothing of him from the paintings and my few memories. A man with a soft, silky beard— a man with a long brush in his hand—a beautiful, entrancing brush tipped with bright, bright red. And then he became Mother's legend. There was a clue there—there should be a clue that ran through all the tangle of lives and ambitions—but I had not Carlo's comprehension. Nevertheless I was glad I had gone to Maremmah. The photographs had come out very well—perhaps Mother could use the brickworks, after all. Then my mind returned to the first spiral—the spiral that had crossed my own—and I wondered whether the sloughing of the house on Sixty-second Street did not also mark an end.

But there did not seem to be an end when I next saw Violet Shore. It was at the wreck of a once historic dance—a dance people had come to in carriages, in the days of diamond tiaras and long dinners and canvasback duck. My old cousin, Antwerp Dyer, had got me the invitation, and I went to please him. It had touched me to meet him again and find that he was still concerned about my mother's first marriage but resolved to be civil to a relative nevertheless. He spoke of my mother as one speaks of a flighty, charming girl— and again I saw Kitty Antwerp, with her long fan in her hand.

All his life he had served and believed in a strange thing called Society, and his faith was unshaken still. And yet I found his company restful, after that of the smooth-faced men. The old apartment house with the big rooms and the creaking elevator had once been "bachelor flats," but the neighborhood had gone down. "I really must move," he would say. "But it's such a nuisance. And then, you know, when you move, Gareth, people are careless. They forget where you are. I might miss an important engagement. And I shouldn't like to do that."

So he lived in the squalling street and was intensely courteous to the large-busted women with string bags whom he met in the elevator. They treated him with a mixture of awe and incredulity, and I think they may have been right. He was a thoroughly selfish man, and he had spent his life in going out to dinner, in going to the opera, in putting studs in a shirtfront and taking them out again. Now the gold shanks were worn and the invitations few, but he preserved certain scruples and a certain finish. It was worn, like the studs, but genuine. With it went a small, flawed integrity —there were some things, such as his name, which he could have sold and had not. For, in the last analysis, his passion for Society was almost selfless —he was perfectly willing to have it kill him or forget him if it did so within the limits of the code to which he subscribed.

I only knew him to show real rancor once, and that was about Ward McAllister. "A pushing fellow," he said. "A very pushing fellow." He spoke of him in the present, as old men will. I asked him about the Mortons. "Oh, they're very responsible people," he said. "The present Mrs. Morton has been a great aid, on the committee. Of course, I know less about that than I did. But they say she is very responsible. Naturally, no one can replace Mrs. Astor. But I know the

Mortons, of course—for that matter, I knew Mr. Shore."

I stared at him, and he must have seen the stare, for he coughed and went on, politely.

"Yes," he said. "Of course you knew him, as well—I remember your saying so. Not very social, naturally, but a remarkable man." He smiled at some recollection. "I met him in the West, years ago," he said. "When I was just out of college. Your dear great-uncle Josiah wished me to take an interest in business, but I am afraid I was rather unsuited to it. Still, the West had its fascination for any young man in those days, and I was glad to go there. It was quite an experience, you know—a rough place, and they had rough ways. Now I believe there are branches of the Junior League in almost every Western city. It must have made quite a difference."

"I can imagine it," I said. "Quite a difference from Mr. Shore's time."

"Oh, yes," he said, blinking. "Mr. Shore. Long Jim Shore, I believe they called him, then. They told me, when I got there, that he was one of the persons I should see. Well, we spent some time together—he was not—ahem—married at the time. I remember his breaking the man's arm, at the mine—the man had attempted to draw a knife. I had not imagined that he was so quick, but he could move very quickly. I had seen very little physical violence, and I hardly realized it had happened till it was over. Then I knew I must have heard the bone snap, and it made me feel faint, for a moment. Mr. Shore was dusting off his hands—he did not seem angry at all. He was a young man, at the time, but he seemed very mature, to me. The man made various threats, but of course nothing came of them—Mr. Shore was quite justified. I asked him why he did not have the fellow arrested, and he said, 'Well, Dyer, arresting a man out here makes a good deal of hard feeling. And I wouldn't want to hurt his reputation, you know.' I've often wondered just what he meant by that."

"Tell me more about it," I said, like a schoolboy, and he looked gratified.

"Well, well," he said. "Let me see. It was all very colorful, of course—and the clear air—yes. I think Mr. Shore himself impressed me as much as anything. There were a good many blustering fellows about—and he could bluster himself, when he chose. But there was a difference—he was quieter than the others and—it seems foolish to say deadlier, I suppose. It was like a new world to me, Gareth, I assure you. He was a striking-looking person—not handsome, but his hair was very black and he moved with the quickness of a pugilist. He drank, as they all did, but it didn't seem to affect him. I recall his saying, 'Oh, I've tried being a hell-raiser. But there isn't enough in it—not compared to getting your hands on something.' He asked me a great many questions about the East—one could feel he was putting the answers away in his mind. I never became very intimate with him, even when he was drinking, but I think he felt he had a destiny and had abandoned some things for it. It's an odd thing to say," he said, and his face was puzzled, "but I imagine he was happier at that time, and shortly afterwards, than he was again. Or perhaps happiness isn't the word —it really isn't the word for a man like that. But he —er—fitted the place and the time. He was in the full stream of it, so to speak—and, well, it was all fantastic. Fantastic—extraordinary—rough." He shook his well-brushed white head at a memory he was unable to put into words.

"Of course, I met him again, when they came to New York," he went on again, briskly, after a moment. "Mrs. Shore was a pretty, scared little thing—she'd improved his grammar, however. I liked her, genuinely—but it's difficult, with all one's obligations. Still, I did what I could—she was not the sort of woman one could launch, unfortunately. I think he realized that, yet he never married again. A hostess is such a help. I don't know that he was pleased with my remembering him—but I may be imputing something that didn't exist. I saw very little of him after Mrs. Shore's death—well, he was a very busy man, as you know. He only alluded to our previous meeting once, in the later years—it was at a dinner at the Harvesters' and we were just about to join the ladies. He'd just formed American Copper and, naturally, most of the men were quite interested. He took my arm, just as we were leaving the dining room, and said, 'Well, Dyer, it's the same sort of game they ran at Fat Louie's, isn't it? Only they talk politer and use prettier chips.' He meant it humorously, of course, but I was rather shocked. Fat Louie's was a rather disreputable place—and they were important men. After all, he belonged to good clubs, before he died. Still, I took his advice and bought the stock—I wish I'd always had such good advice, but one cannot be bothering busy men. You didn't go to the Morton wedding, did you? She made a very lovely bride, though there were criticisms of her manner. But she has shown a real interest, since, and that means so much. I go to few weddings nowadays—I'm rather sorry—they can be such beautiful spectacles, if the family chooses."

He sighed, and I knew that I had no business to go to the dance. But I went.

I went in an ugly mood, for my project seemed to be succeeding, and I had received a letter from Mrs. Vane. It was not the sort of letter one should receive. The hints were as broad as an axe blade, and they concerned her daughter. I did not believe them, but, for a moment, when I thought of them, I did not care. Perhaps Caroline and I would be better apart—and the children had always been hers. I knew the fellow of the hints, and he was as decent as most of us—decent in the Charles Morton way. If it had been Charles Morton himself, the comedy would be complete, I thought savagely. But life was not as neat as that. As for me, I had chosen my rôle and I would play it. I would be the American adventurer to the end.

I dined by myself at a speakeasy and, when it grew late, I still sat there. I was not drunk, but I did not wish to move. I did not wish to do anything. It seemed to me as if, after all the struggle and the passion, I had come to a closed room in life. I could sit there as long as I liked, and it was not unpleasant, but there was no way out. There was no way out because there was no significance. I was neither an artist nor a business man, neither American nor European. I had done a great many different things that came to no end in particular, and I was forty-two. I did not feel like starting them over again.

I looked at my face in the mirror across the room as I had, years ago, in the Vienna express. It was neither bad nor good. Gareth Grant, the well-known dealer and connoisseur. Gareth Grant had begun to go downhill, but that did not show in the face. I thought of the army revolver in the kitbag at my hotel. When you looked down a revolver barrel, it was like a little dark well. It would be exceedingly messy, but one would cease to sit in the closed room. I told myself, reasonably, that I had great cause to live, but I could not feel the cause. I had lost something in youth and made

[*223*]

money instead. I knew the works of the dead, but I no longer saw them with interest. At the end was a closed room, and nothing to say.

Then I found myself giving a white card to a doorman and saying my name.

I realized, when I entered the ballroom, that it was late. I also realized that I would have no one to dance with—at least till I found my cousin— but I was willing to observe. The ballroom itself was ornate—James Shore would have felt at home in it and Kitty Antwerp found it very new and splendid. The jewels were real on the throats and hands of the women—there was a grey mustache and a ribbon across a shirtfront—a foreign dress uniform and a little jingle of medals—and there were the faces of the young, the inheritors, pink, smiling, and healthy. The boxes seemed well filled —from one of them an old lady used a lorgnette. And yet there was something wrong.

There was something wrong with the music: it hurried and wailed, and the saxophone laughed aloud. The laugh did not fit the room, it came from a paper jungle where blacked-up people danced by a limelight moon. The music did not fit the room, the beat was too hasty, too careless, it didn't care who you were but only if you could dance. And, most of all, it was obvious that the inheritors did not fit the room.

"Let's sneak and go over to the Astor," said the tall immaculate boy in tails to the girl with the green feather fan. "This party's dead on its feet."

"I'll have a hot time with Mother," said the girl, doubtfully. "She's parked in a box with a couple of old dodos from Philadelphia, but she's got an eye like a detective."

"Now, beautiful," said the tall boy, "be your age."

They passed by me on their way to the door. I found my cousin at last, alone in the box that had been lent him. He looked tired.

"Well, Gareth," he said, "I hope you have been enjoying yourself. There's nothing quite like it, is there?"

"No," I said. I looked across to another box where a large and smooth-faced man poured drinks into glasses under the table from a flask. He laughed with mechanical heartiness, and the sound of his laugh was sharp. The emeralds on the woman beside him were too large to be false.

"Who are they?" I said. My cousin looked slightly ashamed.

"Those must be the Carvers," he said, briskly. "Motor people, you know. But they're living in New York now. One must have new blood, of course."

"Of course," I said. He looked at me sharply. "People tone down," he said. "Mrs. Astor was very wonderful, of course. But I still remember how we felt about some of the early Steel men. Well, well, their sons are here. It's quite a cycle."

I led him carefully into paths of reminiscence, and he revived. He did not see the young people drifting away—he would not see them drinking gin out of paper cups in the washroom. He would go home and put his program away with the other programs—the dance cards and dinner cards and opera listings of fifty years. He would die still thinking New York existed as a society. And, in that, he would be happy. But I wondered about Violet Shore.

I had seen her, of course, from the moment I entered the room—it was the center box. There was always a stir about it, and people coming and going. She was very beautiful, I thought, and the jewels became her. It was her box they went to, now. Then I knew that the tall boy in tails was her son.

It was not as becoming a fashion to her as the fashions of her youth. But the neck rose from the white shoulders with the old straightness—the lift of the head was the same. And yet there was a change, and not merely a change of Time. The competent, smiling mask had grown part and parcel of the flesh. It was no longer a mask but an essential element. She was very splendid, but she had conquered her beauty at last. The wildness of it was gone.

I stared at the face again, the face unconscious of my eyes. I was sober now, and, as I stared, something frozen within me began to melt away. She had conquered the Mortons, she had conquered her city. But, even as she had conquered, the conquest itself dissolved, for she had come too late. James Shore would not come from the West again, and no one hand would rule New York. There would be a good deal of conquest still for Mr. and Mrs. Carver—but they were other folk. They wanted less than empire, and they would pretend they were doing a service while they acquired it. James Shore and his daughter had been harder metal, and they had not had those particular pretenses.

And yet she was barely forty. I was little over forty myself.

I looked back at my cousin and saw that his head was nodding. I wanted to go away, I wanted to think. The dance floor was thinning out. I roused him, inconspicuously, and excused myself. He seemed a little dazed.

"So pleasant of you, Gareth," he said. "No, no, I think I'll stay for a little. One is always interested in the young people." He straightened his lapels and I left him, staring out alone, at incomprehensible youth and the faces he no longer knew.

On the way out I passed, deliberately, in front of the Morton box. Charles Morton was there, hale, ruddy, and vital—the heavy, boyish face turned animatedly toward a slim dark girl in red. She was young, her hands were uneasy with youth and her body restless, but her face was older than her hands. It had a calculated softness as she listened to the man at her side. Behind the softness the eyes were hard with triumph. I wondered who she was, but it did not matter. All his life Charles

Morton would look for that calculated softness, as a refuge from incalculable reality, and yet go back, in the end, to the woman who was stronger than he.

That woman was talking gayly to the tall grey-haired notability with the diplomatic eyes. He was obviously weary, but he gave her the attention the Latin always gives beauty, deliberate, appraising, and satisfied. As I passed, she turned her head for an instant, and her eyes caught mine. I made the slightest nod of salute, and she smiled. It was a beautiful smile, for it was full recognition. Then her diplomat spoke and she answered, and I passed on.

I got my coat and hat from sleepy attendants and turned, as I thought, toward the elevators. But I must have turned the wrong way. I found myself going down a long corridor with a strange little procession ahead of me—a white-haired woman in an old-fashioned evening dress with high, puffed sleeves, between a motherly person in house-keeper's black and a younger, more worried girl. The motherly person was saying, soothingly, "There, there, dear, straight ahead. Sure the dance is all over and Miss Elsa'll be coming for you."

"But it isn't over—I can still hear the music," said the white-haired woman, sharply. "You mustn't tell lies, Mrs. Ryan. That's naughty. And I haven't seen my dear brother—I haven't seen . . ."

Her voice rose sharply, and she stopped in her tracks. There was a mutter from the motherly person, and a subdued argument. I stepped by them, intending to go on.

"There," said the white-haired woman. "There's someone. He'll tell us." She lifted her head. "Young man, will you kindly tell me if the dance is over?"

I turned, with the blank face we all put on for scenes. Then I felt it change.

"Yes, Aunt Amy," I said, as casually as I could. "The dance is over. I'll get your carriage now."

She looked at me in bewilderment for a moment. Then a strange and painful light came into her face.

"Oh, you know me," she said. "You know me! And yet you're not Aleck—you're not one of James's friends."

"I used to play with Aleck," I said, speaking carefully. "It was in the house. With the railroad

[*230*]

train. The cars were yellow and black, and you said we made a great deal of noise."

"Yes, yes," she said. "A great deal of noise." The motherly person was making mouths at me. I took the frail arm and began to talk steadily, as we moved on. Amy Flower seemed to listen. We passed through a service door and into another corridor. An elevator was waiting.

"You can go, Miss Reed," said the motherly person. "If this gentleman'll be so good. He knows the lady."

"Of course," I said. The younger girl disappeared. I continued talking.

"Why are we going down?" said Miss Flower. "Oh, yes, of course we go down. My brother is down. You said so."

"Just a little lie-down in my room till Miss Elsa comes," crooned the housekeeper.

"Don't want Elsa. Naughty Elsa," said Amy Flower. "Want Mary. Oh, Mary, Mary, my sister —James, my brother—where are you?" Her voice rang in the narrow coop of the elevator. The motherly woman wiped the sweat from her face with a handkerchief. "Watch your step, please," said the elevator man in a professional voice. He was dressed in a blue uniform and looked tired with the night. He was the sort of man who would not have turned his round, bullet head to look at a comet.

"Thanks, Fritz," said the housekeeper as we stepped out. "I'll be seeing you."

"It's O.K.," said Fritz, dispassionately. The door clanged on his incurious face. I do not know where we went, because I was very busy talking, but it was not far. The motherly woman fumbled with a key. "Glory be to God," she said, softly, as we entered the small, overheated room with the red plush furniture and the photographs on the mantelpiece. She shut and locked the door. "Oh, glory be to God," she said again, in a whisper.

"This isn't my brother's room," said Amy Flower. "He has bigger rooms. They took down his house to worry me, but they didn't fool me. I knew he'd be at the hotel—he always stayed there on his trips. I came here with Mary and I had a lovely room. 'Are you comfortable, Amy?' he said. 'The sky's the limit, you know, for Mary's sister.' That was the way he talked. We made a handsome couple when we were dancing, but he liked Mary best. Dear, dear, he liked Mary best. He told me to call him brother."

"Now, Miss Amy," said the motherly woman with sudden authority, "it's time you lay down. Miss Elsa will be cross."

"Cross?" said the old woman with as sudden a docility. "I've been a very good girl. But I'll lie down. I'm tired."

They disappeared into the bedroom together, and I waited. After a while the motherly woman reappeared.

"It's not the sound sleep, but it's something," she said, softly. "I've not even took off her shoes. I'm weak as a cat." She sank into a chair but kept her eyes on the bedroom door.

"Will she try the window?" she murmured. "No, she's not the strength to open it. Well, thank God for you, sir, though I don't know who you are."

"My name's Grant," I said. "I did know her." The woman nodded.

"Sure, I heard you telling her," she said. "You couldn't have made it up. The marvel is how she got dressed and out and all with a nurse in the next room. I'll say this for that Mrs. Sunding—it wouldn't have happened with her by. But Miss Amy was always one for the dances."

[*233*]

She shook her head. "It's God's providence I was on night duty," she said. "'Take me to Mrs. Ryan, the housekeeper. She knows me,' she says, as bold as a duchess, when they turned her away at the door. Well, there's still some men in the hotel that can tell a lady. And hadn't I been second maid in the house and didn't she come to see me regular every year before her trouble? Well, I couldn't abide that she wouldn't see the dancing, she spoke of it so gentle and reasonable. But, sure, the minute she saw it, she wanted to go on the floor. I got her away from that, thanks to Emily Reed, but would she go back the way she'd come? She would not. Has it only been an hour she's been here? It seems like the ages of time. I've had them call the apartment every three minutes and phoning Elsa Sunding all over New York."

A buzzer sounded at the door. She got wearily to her feet.

"And that'll be her, please God," she said. "Well, if she says a black word to me, I'll jump down her throat, for I've done my best."

It was Elsa Sunding, and she did not say the black word, though the air prickled between the two women. She went directly to the bedroom, and in a few minutes I heard a voice say, "Oh, Elsa, dear! I'm so glad you've come. The horrid people wouldn't let me go to the dance."

"There's gratitude for you!" muttered Mrs. Ryan with an indignant shake of her skirt.

So I found myself riding uptown with Miss Flower and her warden. It was necessary, for Aunt Amy refused to release my arm when I tried to hand her in to the car. "Do you mind?" signaled Elsa Sunding, and I gestured "No." It was a quiet trip, for Aunt Amy dozed. Once she woke and said distinctly, "Naughty Garry. Naughty Garry in Paris. Tell James about naughty Garry," but I made no sound. I wondered about the head of the chauffeur of the car. But it, too, was an incurious head.

At the door of the sedate apartment house, Elsa Sunding hesitated. "I'm afraid I shall have to ask you to come up," she said. "I am not sure the nurse is there." Again I gestured my willingness. The night-elevator man gave Elsa an abashed stare and started to mutter something. She froze him and we ascended. I admired her ruthless competence. I wondered where she had been when the call reached her. She was part of the intricate web

[235]

of the Mortons now—and yet I felt sure that, somewhere within that web, she led an entire life of her own.

When we had Aunt Amy safely inside the apartment, there ensued, for me, another period of waiting. The living room was large and beautifully furnished—I wondered what there was about it that struck me as odd. Then I noticed that the windows were double and that nothing in the room was easily breakable or sharp.

Elsa Sunding came into the room. There were stains under her eyes, and the lines in her face were deeper than I had ever seen them, but she was perfectly composed.

"She is resting," she said. "It will be all right now. She has not even caught cold."

I must have looked something in reply, for she shrugged her shoulders.

"What can one do?" she said. "One must always preserve the life. I shall have to be here a great deal now. Mrs. Morton did not think it necessary, but she is wrong. And yet the nurse had good references. Well, she will not nurse again. That is a little too stupid—first to sleep, then to run away. I shall talk to Mr. Morton myself." Her eyes blazed.

"She was probably scared to death when she found Miss Flower had—left," I said.

"So?" said Elsa Sunding. "It is not the business of a nurse—to be scared to death. You must understand, Mr. Grant," she went on earnestly. "It will go for months without disturbance. We drive in the Park and she is very happy—she does not even want to get out and play with the other children. It is only when my orders are disobeyed——"

She paused, as a soft buzzing came at the door.

"That will probably be Mrs. Morton," she said. "I left a message. Well, it is just as well. You will stay here, please, Mr. Grant. You can also explain."

She left me again, and I heard a door opening and low voices for an interminable time in the hall. I felt ill at ease, but I did not intend to go.

The big man came directly toward me, hand outstretched. "We'll drop ceremony, Grant," he said, and all the physical charm I had known so many years before was still in the gesture, though the body was heavier now. "Of course I remember you. Well, we're very grateful."

I said such things as I could say.

"Mrs. Morton will want to thank you herself," he said. "She's with her aunt." He shook his head. "Poor old lady. Can't understand how it happened. You just ran into her by accident?"

We sat down and I gave my account. He listened, now and then breaking in with questions. He had the habit of command now, the regal habit of short words and impressive silences. But it did not grate on me. It is curious, but I felt neither abashed nor envious to be sitting there beside him. I merely felt a vague friendliness and a certain pity. For all his mask of power, the man was obviously hard-worked and disquieted. He, too, was caught in the spiral and not easy with it, in spite of all the complaisant softness that he found, at times, on his road.

We turned from Aunt Amy to the results of the presidential elections, with which he seemed heavily pleased. Things were going to be all right now, with no nonsense about idealists or leagues of nations. The war boom was over—the times depressed—but confidence and sound leadership would triumph. The house that is money rebuilt itself as I listened and climbed further and further toward the skies. The right men were in the saddle, and the horse was eager to be ridden. America had conquered the world; it only remained to consolidate the conquest.

He stopped suddenly, his big hands on his knees. "I'm tired," he said, like a child. "I wish Mrs. Morton would come."

She came, in the jewels and the dress. It was queer to take that warm hand again, not in love. After one glance at his face she said, "Take the car and go home, Charles. I may stay here all night. If I don't, Mr. Grant will see me home."

"Rather rough on Grant," he said. "He's probably just as tired, if he went to that infernal dance. I thought we'd never get away."

She turned on him the full battery of her charm. "I know, Charles. That's why it's so nice of him to stay. Oh, don't be silly, Charles"—as he protested again. "You know you've a meeting tomorrow. I don't have to get up at eight. Send Malden back here for me if you like, and use Jenks in the morning. I probably won't be long, but I'd feel better about it . . ."

He gave me one of those smiles that men give men.

"Marching orders," he said. "Well——" He

turned at the door. "Over here for long, Grant? We might have lunch."

"I'm sailing for England in a very few days," I said.

"Well," he said, "if you should have the time— see about it, will you, dear? We're both very much in your debt, you know . . ."

He went. Violet and I regarded each other when she had come back from the door.

"I can go, if you'd rather be quiet," I said.

"Oh, no. It's a queer meeting, isn't it, Garry? Well, most of our meetings are queer. I just didn't want to discuss it in the car. It would have kept him awake, and that's bad for him. He hasn't been as well as he looks." She smiled, wearily. "Besides, I wanted to see you. How long have you been here, Garry?"

"Six weeks or so," I said. "On business."

"Six weeks and sailing in a few days. Your voice has got very English, Garry. I knew you were married. She must be very pretty and young. And you have children. Girls or boys?"

"Two boys," I said. "They're quite small."

"We have three children," she said. "James is nearly six now. Charles is a freshman at Harvard.

[*240*]

Susan will come out in two years. Did Elsa tell you all that?"

"Not about the other little boy," I said, in a level voice. I thought—if we had had a child he would have been older. The thought was no longer possible.

She smiled, and the smile was secret. The jewels lay cold and glittering on her breast.

"He's a very nice one," she said. "I owed him to Charles, I suppose, but it doesn't seem like that. I wish Father could have seen him."

"He'd have liked to see you tonight," I said because it was true. Her face flushed with pleasure.

"Yes," she said, with the simple arrogance of a child. "Everybody was there. I went over the lists very carefully. It isn't easy, you know, Garry."

"I imagine it isn't," I said.

"And then poor Aunt Amy—well. There'll be backstairs gossip, I suppose. But it doesn't matter." She shook it off with a straightening of her shoulders. "Oh, Garry, there's so much to say and no time ever to say it! Do you suppose there will ever be time?"

"When we're old," I said. She thought, "Yes, I

suppose when we're old. I don't know that I'll like that." Again it seemed to me that she wiped something deliberately from her mind.

"I hated you for a while," she said, in a low voice. "But that's over. And then I hated myself, but you can't do that. It was good for me, though. Before that, I'd always known that it was all Charles' fault. I didn't want to know that it ever could be mine."

"My dear, my dear," I said.

"Oh, no," she said. "Don't protect me. It was fair. But I still don't see how people can take love so lightly. I think love's a very cruel thing. It frightens you—not to be yourself—to be part of someone else. There ought to be something besides that."

It was a last, a passionate cry of that nature which should have been possessed by splendor and greatness and had only found men like Charles Morton and myself. I wondered how to tell her that it still was not too late—not for love but for life. I wondered how to tell her that her empire did not exist, that James Shore was dead. Then I knew there was nothing to say. Her face went back to the mask.

"I wish you could have really seen Charles," she said. "He's tired tonight—he doesn't like trouble. But they're handling big things now. Charles' father was so cautious. He just waited for eggs to hatch." Something naked looked, for a moment, from her eyes. "I've made Charles do it," she said. "Go ahead to the big things, I mean. I wasn't going to lose that. It's hard, in a way, I suppose—he'd be happier, racing his boats—he's quite a good sailor. But, if they don't know their responsibilities, I know them."

The transformation was complete, the metal had taken its final form. It was the price of the conquest —we hadn't known, when we were children, there would be a price. She'd kept her word—she hadn't broken under the weight of the treasure. There were the American duchesses and the women who married and married—she wasn't one of those. But the conquest had taken everything but the strength. And she herself had accepted the thing she conquered.

"Some time I'll send you a picture," I said, lightly. "Or do you like pictures? I forget."

"I like real things better," she said. "But send it. I'd like to have something." She smiled a little.

[*243*]

"And yet I love Charles," she said. "I'm worried when he has a cold."

"I love my wife," I said.

She turned on me the undaunted mask of her face.

"You were talking about pictures," she said. "We changed the house at Morton's Hook five years ago. You can look at a hill from my window now—I made Charles leave it alone. It looks strong, in the winter, when there aren't any leaves on the trees. It's quite far off, but we own it, and I wouldn't have them cut anything or make any paths. Send me something like that, if there is something. I like to look at it. I wish I could be buried there. But the children would think it was queer. After all, it doesn't matter." She lifted her head. "I've thought a great deal about Father," she said, "this last year. He was happy, wasn't he, Garry?"

I found the same difficulty my cousin had in thinking of that particular word in connection with James Shore.

"I don't know if that had much to do with him," I said slowly. "He did what he meant to do."

"Yes," she said, with a sigh of relief. "He did what he meant. That's why I couldn't understand his dying. If he'd only lived till now—there's so much he could have done. More than Morgan, more than anyone. Charles—young Charles—talks about socialism. Well, all boys go through phases. But he doesn't realize. It's people like Father who make the country, not the cranks."

It was the old voice—the voice that had said from the death bed, "My name's Jim Shore and I'm running this." I realized, suddenly, that I no longer subscribed to it, if I had ever wholly sub-scribed. And yet I saluted a certain quality in it—and something that had gone into my veins when I saw my first great engine at the head of the long, disheveled train. Already it was an anachronism —the new men would steal and cheat, but not as James Shore and his like. I had seen them in their offices. The salt had gone out of them, and, with it, some of the grimness. They preferred being imita-tion gentlemen and paper Napoleons. They would pyramid company upon company and pay paper off with more paper till at last, in the secret center of the vast and flimsy maze, sat a smooth-faced, fidgety little man with the eyes of the petty swindler—a rabbit, whom the worship of the Allan Barkers had made a god for a while. But Violet knew only the one doctrine.

The walls of the closed room fell from around me. Something was finished, and beyond it was life.

"I'd like to see young Charles some time," I said. "But I wouldn't worry, my dear. It's quite safe."

She frowned a little, as she always did when she thought.

"I don't very much," she said. "But there isn't much time to be alone. Well, I suppose there'll be time."

She rose, and I took her hands.

"It's too bad, not to meet," I said. "But I suppose we'll have to. All the same——"

"All the same," she said. She raised the linked hands to her lips for a swift instant, and I felt the light kiss. It was brief and untouched as a child's, and I remembered the first kiss I had given her, as a child. Now she had given it back and the circle was shut.

"Never die at all, my dear," she said. "Never die at all."

Then the hands released, and I went for her cloak and my coat.

"Wait," she said, as we went down the hall. "I just want to see——"

She opened a door. A small night light burned by the bed, but Aunt Amy slept soundly. There was even a trace of color in her cheeks, and her face was blind and quite youthful now the eyes were shut. In a chair, by the light, sat Elsa Sunding, reading. The light was very dim, except on her book, but I could just make out the gay Mother Goose pattern brightly stenciled on the wall. The two women who were awake exchanged a long glance, and Elsa Sunding nodded. Then Violet shut the door.

We said little, going back in the car. Once Violet said, "I never met your brother. I wish I had."

"I think he was a great man," I said. "The only one I've ever known."

She frowned a little again.

"I read his novel," she said. "He knew that, too, didn't he, Garry—that love is a cruel thing?"

"Yes," I said. "He had reason to know it, though he was happy."

"He knew something else, too," she said. "He knew that we can't do everything. But I think that's harder to learn."

[*247*]

We shook hands formally at the door for the benefit of her chauffeur. She offered to send me back to my hotel, but I said I'd walk. The iron and glass of the door shut behind her, and I turned away. The light was grey, watery, and indecisive; the long car, as it rolled away, looked black and sleek, like a beast that has just come from a drinking pool, in the mist before dawn. I buttoned the collar of my overcoat—the air was sharp—and walked slowly toward the Avenue. I could see her, going quietly up the great stairs of her house and into the room at last. Charles Morton would be asleep, he would not hear her come in. She could take off the jewels and the dress. Tomorrow there would be many things again—all the telephone bells and the faces, all the vast machine that took up the room of life. But first she would sleep, for a while.

I turned down the empty Avenue. I remembered it crowded with carriages; that would not happen again. Already the buildings looked as if they wished to walk into the Park. I thought of James Shore's daughter. All my life I had misjudged her, from a memory of early love. I had done so in worship and in anger, but I had done wrong. She

[*248*]

was neither a goddess nor an enemy, but mortal woman, briefly alive on an inexplicable planet and bound to betray and be betrayed. And yet, as I thought of her asleep, the old wound ached for the last time—the wound of memory. I remembered the face of Paris, the face of the old half-dollars, youthful and a little stern. They had wasted her, and she had wasted herself, but that was not all or the end. Then the great dream passed like a cloud—the dream of empire. There was an empty street and my steps, ringing. Behind me, to the north, was the Museum—I would go there, today or tomorrow, and see where they had hung the Greco, for I could see it clearly now, and it was more than paint or the money that bought the paint.

The lobby of the hotel had the bare, desolate look they have when the carpets are rolled back and the vacuum cleaners snuffle under the sofas. The cleaning women were busy—the women with pails and mops—the women whose wrists are always red and cold. I rang a long time for the elevator while certain things hardened in my mind. They could get someone else for their affairs—I was done with the adventurer's pattern. I would sail

[*249*]

for England the end of the week, as I had told
Charles Morton. I had one responsibility left, to
the girl I had married and the children I had
begotten, and it might be too late for that. But,
at the least, I could try, for it was a human thing.

When I got to my room I dug the revolver out
of my kitbag and looked at it. I knew now why
I had saved it all this while—it was not as a
souvenir. Suddenly it seemed to me a very stupid
object. It was not even an argument, it was not
an end. Life went on forever and ever, in acts, in
words, in memory, in the strangely compounded
flesh. The one unpardonable sin was to perish, still
in the flesh. It had almost happened to me, but
it would not, now. Then I found myself laughing
at my own grandiosity and the little man in all of
us who shakes his fist at the skies. Yet there was
something I liked in the little man.

I sat down to write to my wife. I would get there
as soon as the letter, in all probability, but I wrote
till the hard dawn came enormously over the rigid
city and my desk light was weak and stupid and
only an imitation of the sun.

PART V

Aɴᴅ yet there are one or two things I must add
to my picture, for nothing is ever finished while
people go on living, and sometimes after that.

When the heaven of the Allan Barkers collapsed
in 1929, I thought of James Shore, and when the
man shot himself in Paris and the cable wires of
the world grew frantic I thought of him again.
But I had the most time to think of him, on my
trip to California and back, in the summer of 1933.

I had not intended to go to California—we were
busy enough, in both New York and Maremmah,

trying to keep alive. But I received a long and excited cable from Mother about a film company, and when I talked to their New York office they immediately put me on a train. At the age of eighty-three, Mother had unexpectedly produced a novel called *Wild Lavender*, so completely Victorian in tone, manner, and substance that some of the most authoritative young reviewers spoke respectfully of a new departure in style. It contained a missing will, a false marriage, a flood, and even an idiot, but it was fatally readable once one got past the initial shock of the first sentence, "The sun was rising in his customary splendor over the little hamlet of B——". Somehow, that first sentence rather stunned the critics—after that, they wrote of the book like men under the influence of a strong and unaccustomed anesthetic. It became a best-seller before they even had a chance to reconsider—and then there was nothing to be done.

Mother was simply delighted. She had never been really jealous of the slow growth of Carlo's fame, but she had begun to speak a trifle bitterly of "these *clever* young men with novels" and "this sex-mad age." As a matter of fact, I seldom read a book where sex is more omnipresent than *Wild Lavender*, in a perfectly nice way. Even the adverbs are female in the little village of B—— But I'm sure that Mother never thought of it in those terms.

I didn't particularly want to be her agent, and neither did her publishers—but it happened in spite of either of us, as matters connected with motion pictures will. And, once I got to the Coast, I was glad I had come. I was treated so very politely, especially by people who did not seem to have the slightest idea either who I was or why I was there. It took three weeks to settle certain details, and it could have been done just as well in New York—but it gave me a rest, and, at last, I found myself shooting back across the continent, with everything arranged and the memory of an incredible city where everything was pasteboard, even the taste of the beef. I went back by way of San Francisco, for I wished to see as much as I could and I did not know when I would have the chance again. And then, when I saw the black dot on the railway map and the name beside it, I knew I would have to stop. I knew it had been a pilgrimage, after all.

It gave me a queer feeling to be walking the streets of that high mountain town where James Shore and his fate had met. The streets were paved and lighted now; the stores had their plate-glass windows; the movie theaters blazed furiously at night. In the lobby of the hotel a cabinet radio emitted a voice like canned syrup, and Time struck a bell from Denver while nobody listened at all. And yet, from the moment I got off the train and saw the hard name, "GUNFLINT," picked out in whitewashed stones, I was conscious of a largeness and a desolation—the largeness of a frontier, the desolation of a mining camp when the pay dirt pinches out.

There were men in the streets at the wrong times —the times when men should be working. There wasn't enough smoke from the smelters—it barely tainted the sky. The night was noisy enough, but not with the right sort of noisiness. They'd made the big machine, and now there was nothing to feed it. Copper was eight cents a pound—and the back supply still unbought.

I hadn't been so high since Anderesplatz, and now I was fifty-five. It made my heart beat fast and my breath come short. I didn't mind, particularly, but it gave all things the quality of a dream. The black mountains were like the mountains of a dream, and the air, so cold at evening, seemed at once an intoxicant and a drug. At times I would think I saw James Shore in any one of the big, two-handed men who passed me so gravely and idly in the streets, with the look of lost work on their faces; at times I would find myself almost nodding as I walked. I walked a great deal, though slowly, because of my breath. I saw Mary Shore Park and the Shore Memorial Library, with quiet men, sitting at tables, not even reading, just staring at newspapers. I saw the empty store fronts. And all the time that eeriness went with me—the eeriness of a dream.

The boy who showed me around the Lucky Dollar was a very nice boy indeed. I call him a boy, though I suppose he was thirty. But the youth was still in his face, though it was a bewildered youth. He kept saying, "Of course you're not seeing this under normal conditions" and looking at me rather wistfully, as if my assent would, somehow, fortify a faith. I had telegraphed certain people in New York to make the visit possible—not the Mortons, I did not wish to use their name—and, when we

[*257*]

were done, he invited me to dinner. "The hotel's pretty bad," he said. "It was all right three years ago, but . . ." I assured him I did not mind the hotel.

I lay on my bed in the small hot room—I was tired, after the visit, and he had promised to call for me later—and thought over what I had seen. I had been in mines before, and the mine itself did not interest me particularly, except as one is always interested by the labor and ingenuity of men. And the men out of work I knew. It was more than that which moved in me—more even than the fantastic mountains and the wild air. And yet, when I tried to fix upon it, it shrank to a couple of small, irrelevant facts. It was here that James Shore had made his pile; it was here that he had married and Violet had been born. These things were not important beside the mountains and the labor, but they were important to me.

I could see the place as it had been when he had first come there—the raw, roaring city of shacks and tents where you paid for your drinks in silver and the shifts worked day and night. It must have suited him wholly—it must have been worth the struggle—worth being James Shore. I had always thought of him as ruling the metal, but now I saw the metal ruling him, pushing him, driving him halfway across the continent to the death in Europe at last. It was not Nemesis, but it had served its turn.

I thought of the inheritance. It did not matter about Aleck, for nothing about Aleck mattered very much. I had seen him, by chance, in London, after his third divorce. He looked like a retired policeman, with his chest gone down into belly, though his face, now it was older, bore a stronger resemblance to his father's than it ever had. It was curious, seeing the likeness and hearing the weak words come out of the mouth. He would never know the loot of the mine had destroyed him, he would put it all down to his wives. The son was a gentleman rider who thought his father bad form; the daughters by the second wife were carried along in the train of their mother's marriages; the third wife had been childless, which was as well. He spoke of them all in the voice of a much-wronged man. It was when he began to speak of his sister in that voice that I left him, wishing I had done so before.

[*259*]

The loot had not broken Violet, but it had become part of her flesh. Without it she would not have wished to conquer the Mortons, and because of it, and her father, she had driven Charles Morton on. The combination was a fatal one, given his particular temperament. He had not been stupider or greedier than many of the others, but he'd had to convince himself that he was a gentleman and yet play the potentate. All the partners of Morton and Company were gentlemen at last, and they had played marbles for empire with the solemnity of well-brushed children till a street boy, who knew no rules at all, had joined in the game and taken their marbles away. They had not even been able to punish the street boy, for he had run away into death before they had found him out.

It hadn't been the only mistake, merely the most glaring. But it had been enough, for it was something almost anyone could understand. They had all made a mystery of their calling—not only Charles Morton. There were the great, softly lighted buildings, the secretaries of secretaries, the shibboleths and the slogans and all the priestly hush. And when the raw glare of the photographer's flashlight beat upon it, there was nothing there but stupidity and greed. They had had the management of a nation—the Charles Mortons—and firmly, pompously, and almost automatically they had thrown it out of the window to land forty stories down. Men could forgive greed, and had—men could hate and worship tyranny—but these were not even tyrants. I remembered an advertising scheme I had seen in New York—a parade of great swollen figures, of lunatic balloons in the shape of beasts and men. They waddled the street in pomp—and the end was a sack of painted rubber, in some field, when they were released and the gas gave out. It was a fit symbol—when they waddled the streets, in pomp, the crowd had laughed and cheered.

I remembered a picture of Charles Morton taken, at the investigation, by the raw glare of the photographer's flashlight. He had answered his questions with dignity, he had had the best counsel. All his physical presence and charm had come into play. But one camera had caught him off guard. You saw him between his lawyer and his son, and the face was the face of a schoolboy, confused and surly, thinking it unfair the teacher should ask such hard questions when everybody in school knew that he was good at his games. The son's face was merely incredulous that a dynasty should fall. They had not failed like Jay Cooke, but the new names were already appearing on the board. Charles Morton would take a trip to Europe for his health and return as senior chairman, if all went well. They would let him come to the offices, and he would sign letters for a while. There was still value in the name, and Mrs. Charles Whipley Morton would still be a patroness of hospitals, of organizations, of leagues. That, too, was if all went well. But I suddenly knew that not even Violet could stop the progress of the rock of money, once it had started to roll downhill.

She would fight all the rest of her life and save certain things and die fighting, but she would not prevail, unless James Shore came back to earth again in the flesh of her youngest son. But I had seen that too sensitive face in a picture—the face with the artist's mouth that comes so often at the end of the faces of strong prey—and I did not think it would happen. It would have to be the grandchildren, and, by then, the world might be changed.

Last of all, I thought of myself and my own life. My parents had fled to Europe to follow the torch, but I had come back with my wife. It hadn't been simple to do. But, doing so, I had recovered something of the Caroline I had married, though not easily and after years. I had no mystic belief in the mere virtues of return, but there was something at Maremmah that I hadn't found elsewhere— something more like peace. And, oddly enough, it was so for Caroline, too, for she came of a rooted stock—the stock that will bear transplanting, if there is earth at the end. I had had many doubts and misgivings, but it had worked. I had known it would work when I had showed her Jared Antwerp's house and she'd said, "But, Gareth, you can see where the line of the garden was. They must have grown peaches on the south wall— they'd surely have had a wall." Then, coming back in the train, she'd talked of her own childhood to me, for the first time, and it had been the breaking of a barrier between us. I'd been stupid—I hadn't known how her mother had hurt them all— or how she'd been made to feel afraid.

I thought of my children—already they lived in a different world than mine—that was bound to be so. They were both of us, and neither. But they weren't English and they weren't in exile. At least they didn't seem so. They seemed to me astonishingly competent and decided, for boys. Perhaps they were not—perhaps they would come to nothing. Hugh could make a potter, if he chose —he might not choose. And, always, the airplanes might come and the world end. One had to reckon with that. One thought of it only in flashes, but one had to reckon with it. There had been a shell of safety over my childhood—it was not over my sons. And yet my mother had seen the streets hung with black for Lincoln's funeral—she had outlived four empires, a republic, and countless industries, and I felt perfectly sure that she would die in her bed. Only last week she had received the unofficial congratulations of both Il Duce and the Pope on the excellent moral attitude of *Wild Lavender*. There were such people, and they continued to exist, in spite of systems and wars.

I had neither Carlo's fortitude nor Mother's single-mindedness—but we made good china at Maremmah—and, during the boom, I'd sold some pictures that should have been sold. I had very few delusions about either task. I would always have a streak of the promoter, and most painters would hate me, inevitably. But we'd started Hudson Corbet—as far as any reality can be "started"—and when Martin-Agache came over from Paris, our shop was the first thing he came to. He'd have come to me in the Rue de La Boétie, too, but to see how much he could get. This time, he came to see the work. There was a difference, though there was little point in pretending it was more than a difference. But at least I dealt with the living, not the dead.

And what we made at Maremmah was living also. It was a small business, very small. We could have made it larger during the wild years. But I hadn't, deliberately, and in the face of advice. I wasn't Sir Hugo Isaacstein and I was tired of the pattern of James Shore. As it was, its smallness had saved it—and even made a profit, in the long run. It might smash yet, but I didn't think so. I liked the new plates we'd made—the ones with the Indian design. "Oh, yes, Gareth Grant," I thought, "you'd have to have it a success." But, as I thought it, I chuckled. At least it was a success that Caroline's mother neither understood nor approved.

[*265*]

Elsa Sunding had been one of the people who understood the most. She had come to Maremmah in a limousine at the height of the boom, and I had spent an afternoon showing her around. At the end, she had bought, intelligently and lavishly, for her house in Connecticut. "Oh, yes, Mr. Grant," she had said, "I can afford it. I am really very well off now." I had taken her back to tea, and Caroline hadn't liked her, though the two women had been polite. But, before that, she had said two things—one, as she took up a cup and set it down again—"It is real, Mr. Grant. It feels right. You must be happy."

She looked at the cup again.

"Something to make that is right," she said. "I have nothing but my son, and that is another affair. But I would not change."

She showed me the photograph. The face with the strong mouth had the look of success. He had a fellowship at the James Shore Foundation. I congratulated her.

"He will marry inside three years now," she said briefly. "Maybe less. Well, then, I will still have my house. He will make money, perhaps, but I have not brought him up for that. I have come too long a way to be interested."

[*266*]

"Most people aren't like that, who have come a long way," I said.

She gave me a quick glance.

"Most people are fools," she said. "Oh, yes, I wish to be the mamma of the celebrated. That is true. But I have much patience. I have made him have patience. He will not do certain things."

I believed her, though I would not have wished to be her son. After a moment she spoke again, reflectively.

"One is sometimes possessed," she said. "I will not say by a demon—that is superstitious. But one is sometimes possessed. It was so with me, when I first came to this country. You do not know my history, Mr. Grant, and there is no need nor interest to tell you. But I know what it is—to suffer that possession. One is glad to have escaped—yes —but one does not forget it, either. The man may have been nothing—it was the possession. My God, I was young!" she said violently, "I believed in a great deal. Now I know they were only men and women, but it does not pay back the youth. Nevertheless one makes something, afterward. One would not have made it otherwise, I think." She stopped, and her face changed.

[*267*]

"You will excuse me for talking so much, Mr. Grant," she said. "It is only that a man died last week, in the country where I was born and I read of it. He died very old—oh, much older than Mr. Shore. They will knock three times at the door at the vault, when they put him there, for that is the custom. Bread, salt, and water in a silver dish and the smell of the fresh-cut fir twigs—oh, I saw it when his father went to the vault—I can remember everything that is done. They used to be very powerful, but the times have changed, and the new one, they say, paints his face like a woman, without shame. I wanted to hate, but I could not feel any hate when I read of the death—just that I could stop the papers now. I have taken them for years to read that one thing—it would not be in the American papers, though he was important. Perhaps one should be a religious, but I think that is hard for persons like you and me, Mr. Grant. Or you may be one, of course—after all, I do not know you very well."

"No, I'm not," I said. "I believed in my brother, though."

"Yes," she said. "I saw that, in Vienna. I believe in my son, as you have gathered." She smiled.

"Well, we have both survived, Mr. Grant. That has its importance. It is interesting, to be able to survive." She paused. "Mrs. Morton is well," she said. "But doubtless you saw the last picture—at the anniversary of the Foundation."

"Yes," I said. "She looked well, I thought—rather changed, of course. I have not seen her in a number of years, though her daughter came into the shop once or twice. She bought a couple of etchings, for wedding presents, I think—fairly good ones. I should say she looked more like her father."

"Yes," said Elsa Sunding. "The young one is, perhaps, more interesting. But art is not often made by the too sheltered. Nevertheless I am glad I have known Mrs. Morton. She does not like me, particularly, but we see each other still. They were generous—yes. I shall tell her I have seen you, if you do not mind. Perhaps, some time, you and your wife will stop and see me in Connecticut. It is not a bad house." She paused again. "All my life I have thought, 'When it is over, I will go back to Europe,'" she said reflectively. "But now I know I will not. You are contented here, also, Mr. Grant."

[*269*]

"Contented?" I said. "I'm even getting fat. It astonishes me."

"Well, I am content," she said, as if to herself. "Only sometimes one hears the water at night— the water one drank when one was thirsty, in the youth. They must hear little, at night, the people who make no mistakes. But I don't think they sleep any better for it. I like this pattern very much—is it your design?"

Somehow I felt that she still had her house, in spite of the crash in the world. I could see Violet coming to it, now and again, drawn by the bond that is strong as love or hate, the bond of shared memory. In the end the two old women would sit in two rigid chairs and tartly discuss the failings of the world. It would not matter if either were rich or poor, then, for both had fought with life and carried the wounds.

My young man came for me in his car, and we drove still higher than the town, up a road that crawled the flank of a mountain. The porch of his house looked out over a gulf, and we had cocktails there. As we drank, we saw the astounding sunset and the night fall, with mountain swiftness. There were only the three of us, my host, his wife, and myself, and I had the feeling of an outpost when night had fallen, in spite of the lights that began to wink on in the valley.

"It must be strange, after New York," said my hostess.

"I suppose you're right," I said. "It's as far away as that," and they both laughed.

They were pleasant people, and I hope they enjoyed the dinner as much as I did. My host seemed impressed when he found out that I had known James Shore. But it was a vague awe—he spoke of him as he might of a dead, long fabulous god. I asked if there was anybody left in Gunflint who had known him in the early days.

"Well, let's see," he said. "There's old Clancy, the watchman. He tells all sorts of yarns. But he's such a hearty old liar, you never can tell. Mrs. Beech, the old librarian, knew Mrs. Shore, I believe, but she died last winter. And there's Arkroyd —but he's on a pension—I think they moved to the Coast. If you were doing a book or anything, I suppose the family itself would be the best bet. They've been out of American Copper for years, but Mrs. Morton was born here, you know." Of her, too, he spoke with the respect due to the fabulous, almost with the respect that is due the dead.

"Oh, I'm not doing a book," I said. "But I met him once or twice. And coming here made me remember him."

"There were more old-timers left when I first came here," he said. "They remembered him, I guess. But that was five years ago, and you know how they drop off. What was the name of the fellow who wouldn't believe in the merger—Johnson—Wilson——"

"Ed Jackson?" said his wife.

"Yes, Ed Jackson. He was one of the real old-timers. Hard-rock man from the Washoe and all that. Well, you know how long ago the merger happened—oh, thirty years, anyway. Well, anyhow, when Hard Rock Ed got his first week's pay check, after that, he took it back to the window. 'Take this damn thing back and give me something that's worth money,' he said, 'or I'll crawl into that hole of yours and beat you to death with a pickaxe. I don't know anything about this goddam American Copper,' he said. 'I'm working for Long Jim Shore.'" He laughed. "They were pretty independent in those days," he said. "Well, they still are."

I spoke of the men in the streets, and the lines the cocktails had erased came back into his face. He looked older than I had thought him.

"It's bound to pick up soon," he said stoutly. "The world's got to have copper. When Gracia and I first came here—we thought we'd be going back East in a year or so, vice-president and all that. That was 1928. Well, we've been lucky to stay. I know some of those boom vice-presidents." He whistled. "Anyhow, New York doesn't send us so much hooey about the Spirit of American Copper or what have you. They used to send quite a lot. But I guess they're saving printing bills. Those boys ought to come out here once in a while and see what the country's like!" he burst out. "I'm as hard-boiled as the next guy—shut up, Gracia!—but it's been like watching something die, the last three years!" His wife put her hand on his arm, and he relaxed—the argument was, obviously, an old one.

"I think we've all been watching something die," I said. "I'm not sure that part of it's bad."

"You mean it's better dead?" he said, unexpectedly. "Well, you might be right. Good Lord, when I got out of college . . ."

He went on with his own argument. It was an interesting one, but, while I listened, I let my mind drift back. Other things might survive—the mines and the metal—but James Shore, as James Shore, was dead. There was nothing left, even here, but the lies of a night watchman and a legend already dim. There had been the struggle, the achievement, and the Nemesis. There was nothing left at all.

The buildings of the Shore Foundation rose before me to confute my statement—all the glass and the stainless metal and the white stone. Men looked through metal eyes at a wiggle of life on a slide; they repeated a process a thousand times, and at the end wrote, "Not proven"; now and then they gathered one or two careful facts together in a small, drab pamphlet with an unintelligible title; in the end, because of such actions, the world might be a different world. But if it became a different world, James Shore would be the last to take credit for it. He had not wished it otherwise than it was. It had been in his nature to do what he had done—but he would not have made the Foundation if Aleck had been the strong child.

I could hear the tired voice in my ears, saying, with dry amusement, "Well, they might as well try it, Colonel—as long as the frogs hold out."

No, the statement was not confuted, for all the metal and the stone. The great raid East had failed. I wondered, for a moment, about the shadow named Mary Flower, Mary Shore. It came over me, with an odd shock, that I did not even know where the two were buried. It did not matter greatly. He was not a sentimental man, and one hotel was like another hotel.

We were sitting on the porch now, well wrapped up, for the air was cold. The stars were near and very bright. I thought of nights at Anderesplatz, sitting with Carlo, while together we pieced an America out of the darkness, because he had wished to know. He should have seen this, too. Something was dying, yes, but the country was alive. I was glad I was alive to see it, even if the airplanes came.

I wondered, for an instant, what James Shore's daughter was seeing, on the liner that took her to Europe, with the white-haired, snappish man who still had the schoolboy's scowl when life caught him unprepared. I could see her walking the deck, with her head thrown back, and the meaningless furs of Empire at her throat. She would do that alone, before she went back to the suite at night, and she would not think, for that while. She would never regret, she would never abandon—when the loneliness came, she would be able to bear the loneliness. I could see her very plainly now, though I doubtless made her face younger than it was. I suddenly knew there would never be that last meeting between us, that meeting we all wish for, when everything is explained. And yet, while I lived, I would think of her, not always, but when the heart was shaken by a strong emotion and sometimes for no reason I knew.

I would rest by my wife, in the end, and she by her husband, but that did not alter the case. There was a link between us, and we had changed each other's lives. "Let them make the new world," I thought. "But when they have made it, there will still be men and women, there will still be life." I had gone wrong—as the pioneer impulse had gone wrong in James Shore. And yet I had shared in something.

"So what the hell?" said my host, continuing his argument. "We've got the plant and the methods —we know we can do the work. And yet we're all in a jam. Well, I'm no expert, and I don't care how they fix it, but it's got to be fixed, somehow, whether the old boys admit it or not. There's got to be some sort of change."

I looked out into the darkness, as if from an outpost. The lights in the valley seemed no nearer than the stars. It was all as it had been when James Shore first came here, and yet it was not.

"Yes," I said. "We've ended a time and begun a new one. Some day we'll look back and see it was that. There was a man called Goethe who sat by the Prussian campfires, after the battle of Valmy, and wrote that he'd seen the beginning of a new world. It's hard to live, when that happens. But it has to be."

They had thought it all settled and finished when they built the great machine. But it was not even begun.

THE END

[277]